KARMA

Teresa Hurst

KARMA

Printed in the United States of America

First Printing, 2018

Publishing and Cover Design by:

Hydra Productions
Salt Lake City, UT
657-206-5360

https://www.hydraproductionsonline.com/

Please don't judge too harshly. This is the original version and the editing wasn't the best. Maybe it will be worth some money as a signed first edition one day :)

CONTENTS

DEDICATION

To my amazing husband who has never wavered in his unconditional love and support. You changed everything for me. I promise to kill you in a book one day. I LOVE YOU!!!!!

To Bug and Boo: I'm still here. I love you forever...

Teresa Hurst

ONE

I stood silently in the kitchen, looking at the gift I had placed on the table. The box was wrapped in simple brown paper. *Happy Anniversary* was written in black Sharpie across the top.

There was nothing fancy about the appearance of this gift. I had done that intentionally. I wanted the outside to be boring. It was what was inside the package that was exciting. I smiled thinking about it. Knowing how much relief it would bring to them brought me peace. I haven't had much of that in the last year.

My mind began to wander. The package reminded me of my parents in so many ways. They hadn't been exceptionally good looking, but they were amazing people. They were the type that always surprised you with what they did next. They were fun. They were interesting. They were brilliant. You never would have guessed it by looking at them, though, just like the package on the table.

I thought about the party for my mom and dad's thirtieth

wedding anniversary. It had been a wonderful gathering of the people they loved. All of their friends had been there. I remembered everyone was having a blast. The venue was beautifully decorated in shades of blue and silver just like on the day they had been married. There was an exact replica of their wedding cake. Laughter was the dominant sound throughout the hall. We had karaoke all night because Mom and Dad had a fondness for karaoke bars. The night had been filled with cringe-worthy renditions of classic rock songs. Dad had decided to sing "Stuck With You", and it had been both awful and wonderful. Not a single note had been on key, but the enthusiasm with which he had belted it out had been adorable. Mom had laughed throughout the entire performance then melted into him when he finished. They had been so in love that a blind person could have seen it.

It was a glorious event. Had it not been for what happened afterward, it would have been the type of party people talked about for years to come. Unfortunately, the events that unfolded after the party overshadowed the celebration.

That had been just over a year ago. They never made it home that night.

I couldn't think about them any longer. I snapped myself back into the present moment, and I looked around the small kitchen one last time before silently slipping out the back door, making sure it was securely locked behind me. I didn't want to be proud of myself, but I couldn't shake the feeling.

I walked back to where I had parked my rental car a few blocks over. Along the way, I reminded myself of what my mother always said about good deeds. "It's not a truly good deed if you want to be rewarded or recognized for having done it. You shouldn't expect a thank you for having done what is right." Her words were the reason for my anonymity.

TWO

Mandi walked down the stairs towards the kitchen. She tucked the section of her hair that refused to stay in her bun behind her ear Having been up and moving for almost an hour now, she was already dressed with her hair and makeup done for the day.

She glanced out the window. It was still dark outside, and she could see the dew glistening on the grass. The part of her that was still a child at heart wanted to walk through it barefoot. The adult side of her thought about how much she hated having to be up this early each day. Reaching the bottom of the stairs, she almost tripped over their cat, Pepper. He weaved his way in between her legs as she walked, making it much more difficult for her to walk in her drowsy state. When she got to the kitchen, she started the morning coffee and filled Pepper's food dish. As she turned back around, she noticed a small package, wrapped only in plain brown paper, on the breakfast table. A smile crept across her face, and she rubbed her eyes in an unsuccessful attempt to clear her vision. For once, she thought, Janet hadn't forgotten their anniversary.

Deciding to wait until everyone else was awake to open the present, Mandi went to the living room to grab her laptop. She needed to check her email and look over her schedule for the day. She realized how full this day was going to be and sighed. She had three different meetings scheduled, lunch with a prospective client, and soccer practice with the kids this evening. Muttering to herself about how much caffeine it would take to make it through this day, she got up and began looking for the largest coffee cup she could find. Wrapping her hands around the warm mug, she inhaled the aroma of the coffee. It was one of her favorite smells, and she could feel the aroma begin to bring her to life. She sat back down at the table with her cup of liquid energy and went into auto-pilot answering and sending emails.

As she worked, her thoughts drifted. She thought about starting to look for a new job. Ten years ago, she had loved every minute of being an event planner. The last few years had taken a toll on her previously optimistic outlook on life. She wasn't at the point of being a pessimist, but reality had set in and life was no longer one big party. She didn't hate her job by any means. She was very good at what she did, and she had an excellent reputation for being able to exceed the expectations of her clients. She simply didn't find joy in planning parties for strangers any longer.

None of that mattered, though. She knew that she wouldn't be making any career changes any time soon. They weren't in a financial position to allow her to change career paths at this point. They were making ends meet but only by a slim margin. For a brief moment, she felt an overwhelming sense of sadness because of their financial situation. Their savings were down to nothing. If one of them were to become sick it could be disastrous.

She looked up, and the first thing to catch her eye was a colorful drawing of stick figures hanging on the refrigerator. They all had smiles on their faces, and there was a giant sun hanging in the sky. She smiled, and the sadness immediately faded. No amount of money would ever make her feel better than knowing that the kids were home, and they were safe.

It wasn't until she heard the sound of the bathroom door shutting upstairs that she realized she needed to get breakfast started. Everyone would be downstairs soon. If nothing else in their lives was predictable, their morning routine was. She was always the first one awake. About an hour after she got out of bed, everyone else would start moving around. Janet would take a shower before heading downstairs, and the kids would yell about not liking the clothes that had been laid out for them. She always cooked breakfast. Always. She couldn't imagine starting the day without having that time together around the table each morning. It was her favorite part of the day.

This morning they would be having waffles and bacon. Normally, she would prepare something healthier, but it was Janet's favorite. It was their traditional anniversary breakfast. The kids would be happy about it. She always found it amusing when the kids would ask for cold cereal in place of the cooked breakfast she had prepared. Occasionally, she would cave to their wishes, but most mornings she would make them eat what she cooked. She knew that one day they would appreciate that she had made the effort to cook for them each morning.

Dylan was the first one to make it to the kitchen. At five years old, he never walked down the stairs. He jumped, taking them two at a time. It always made Mandi nervous. She could easily see him misjudging a jump and ending up with a broken arm. He was the type of kid you picture as the youngest son on a prime-time family sitcom. His face was still round, and he was always full of questions that forced you to suppress a laugh before answering. This morning his dark brown hair was sticking up in the back, and Mandi tried in vain to make it lay down. He squirmed at her efforts, saying that he wanted it that way. She didn't argue with him because one of the things she loved most about both of the kids was that they both had such strong personalities. They weren't the type of kids that let others dictate who they were. It was a source of pride to know that they were both so comfortable being themselves.

Dory came down next. She was seven going on seventeen. She had pulled her blonde hair up into high pigtails this morning, one being quite a bit higher than the other. Mandi knew that it was intentional. Dory had chosen not to wear the clothes that had been laid out for her today. She was wearing polka dot pants and socks with emojis on them that were pulled up to her knees. The child had a strange sense of fashion that made her even more adorable. When she sat down at the table next to her brother, Mandi pointed out that her shirt was on backward. The three of them began to laugh as Dory tried to turn her shirt around without actually taking it off. Once she got it turned around, she looked down at the shirt and announced, "I like it better the other way." She turned it back around, and the three of them burst out in a fit of laughter.

"What's so funny in here?" Janet was walking into the kitchen. Her long hair was still wrapped in a towel on top of her head. Her face was still slightly pink from the apricot scrub that she used each morning.

Dylan exclaimed, "Dory forgot how to dress herself!"

"Yeah, well at least I don't look like a peacock!" Dory spit back quickly with a grin on her face. She was proud of herself for the witty retort.

Laughing, Janet walked over and ruffled Dylan's hair. "I guess we're all just a mess this morning. Look! Mama Mandi has a coffee stain on her shirt."

Without even looking down at the stain, Mandi walked over to grab a paper towel. "Well, we may not look like the poster children for Good Housekeeping magazine, but at least we're all here!" She wiped at the stain on her shirt and kissed Janet on the cheek. "Happy anniversary pink cheeks! Should I open my present now or wait until after we eat?"

"Oh, you've got a present? I vote you open the present first. Presents are a great way to start a day!" Janet replied. Mandi wasn't at all surprised by her answer. Somehow, Janet had never lost her child-like love of presents.

Mandi sat down with her family, unable to stifle the smile that was consuming her face. She unwrapped the package, finding a small stack of papers inside the box. There was a card on top that had *Grayson Family* written on the envelope. Mandi's expression went from excitement to confusion in an instant.

Janet immediately noticed the change in Mandi's face. "What's wrong? Why do you look like that?" She stood up and walked to the other side of the table where Mandi was sitting.

"This isn't from you?" It wasn't as much a question as it was a realization. "I thought this was your anniversary present to me." Mandi was baffled.

"Nope, not from me. My present for you is still upstairs. I assumed it was from the kids." A look of concern swept across Janet's face. They both turned to look at the kids.

Dory and Dylan looked at each other and shook their heads. Dory leaned over to look in the box. "It says it's for all of us, but it looks like it's just a bunch of papers. What a boring present! Who gives someone a box of papers for their anniversary?" Dory pouted.

Mandi hesitantly opened the card and read it silently. As she did, tears began running down her face, and she covered her mouth with her hand, barely masking the gasps that were coming involuntarily from within her. Janet grabbed the card from Mandi's hands as Mandi began looking at the stack of papers. As Janet read the card, she put a hand on her chest and also began crying.

Mandi handed the papers to Janet. "Look at this!" The words barely came out. She was in complete shock. "Look at this!" she repeated with more urgency.

Janet quickly looked through the papers. "Is this real? This can't be real, can it?" She was visibly shaking at this point. They looked at each other and began crying even harder. They wrapped their arms around each other and sank to the floor.

Dylan and Dory began crying as well. They were so confused. They didn't know what was going on. All they knew was that their moms were crying, and it made both of them sad and scared. They had seen enough tears in their short lives to know that it didn't usually mean good news when people cried.

"Mama J! What's wrong? Why are you crying? What happened?" Dylan was screeching.

"Oh, my babies! Don't worry! These are happy tears!" Mandi said in the most comforting voice she could muster. "This is just the best present ever, after you two, of course! Someone has helped us out a lot. I don't know who, but they have done something for all of us that will make our lives a lot easier!"

Dory didn't understand. "You don't know who it was? How did they leave the present here if you don't know them?"

Mandi and Janet walked over to their children and hugged them tightly. "I'm not sure, but that's not really important right now. Let's eat breakfast, and we'll tell you what all the papers in the box are about. I think you'll be a bit more excited about them once you know what they are." Mandi felt a peace come over her that she had only felt once before in her life. She finally knew, without any doubt, that her family was truly going to be okay.

THREE

Local Family Receives Gift From Anonymous Benefactor

Janet and Mandi Grayson woke up Tuesday morning to an unexpected surprise. Someone, unknown to the couple, had left a gift-wrapped package on their kitchen table. Thinking that it was an anniversary present from Janet, Mandi opened the gift without hesitation. Quickly realizing that the gift wasn't from Janet, Mandi's excitement almost immediately changed to fear, and then to overwhelming joy. Inside the package, they found a card that explained the papers that were included. The unsigned card stated that they were being given this gift because they deserved some happiness and peace of mind after all the struggles that they had faced in the last couple of years.

If their names sound familiar, it may be because the couple had been involved in a highly publicized custody battle that was resolved recently. Janet's sister and brother-in-law had been tragically killed in a car accident, leaving their two young children as orphans. Janet and Mandi, being the only living relatives of the children, had immediately offered to take the children into their home. The state had fought the placement of the children into the couple's care because of their sexual orientation. For almost two years, the couple endured multiple court hearings, home inspections, and scrutiny of their private lives. Finally, three months ago, the couple was granted full custody of the children. They immediately petitioned the court for the right to legally adopt the children and not simply be their legal custodians. Their petition was granted just last week, and the adoption was finalized.

The couple finally felt like everything was just as it should be. They knew things weren't perfect, but they had no doubt that they could make it through any struggles that might come their way. They had incurred some debt from losing time from work and their extensive legal fees but believed that while things might be tight financially for a while it was all worth it in the end. "We weren't going to be going on any vacations any time soon, but we had our family together, and that was all that mattered to us," Mandi continued, "We definitely weren't expecting this gift! Behind having our family together, this was the second-best thing that has ever happened to us."

The package they received included the clear deed to their house, the keys to two, brand new, fully paid for, vehicles, an undisclosed amount of money deposited into their bank account, utility bills that have been paid two years *in advance, and over one hundred gift cards for various local businesses. "We may never know who did this for us, but I hope that they know that we will try to live our lives in a way that will make them never regret it. Thank you, whoever you are! You have changed our lives forever, and we can never express completely how grateful we are!" Janet said while fighting back tears.*

I truly hoped that they would not face any further hardships. I had been searching for someone to help for months, but the moment I read their story, I knew that they were the perfect family for me. The timing of the gift hadn't been coincidental. I had decided months ago what I was going to do for them. As soon as I heard that the adoption had been finalized, I paid off their debts and gathered the necessary paperwork to give them. My biggest concern had been getting in and out of their house unnoticed.

It was much easier than I had thought it would be. That fact had triggered me to get them one final gift that they would find out about tomorrow. They would be getting a new state of the art security system installed. I wanted them to not only be financially and emotionally set, but I needed them to be physically safe as well.

I didn't want to dwell on my good deed too long, though. I didn't have time to spare. I had another mission to complete, and it wouldn't be nearly as nice as this one had been. "Why so serious this morning?" I jumped at the sound of my housekeeper's voice. I hadn't heard her walk up behind me.

I stood up from my chair at the kitchen counter. "Oh, it's nothing Gayle. I'm just thinking about this next trip. I've got a massive to-do list. Were you trying to scare me out of my skin? If so, you were almost successful!"

"I'm sorry dear. I guess I just assumed you heard these two wrestling their way across the house." She looked down at my dogs who were engrossed in an intense tug-of-war match with a tattered old rope. "I definitely didn't mean to startle you."

I looked down at my dogs rolling around on the floor at Gayle's feet. Seeing the two of them being playful brought a smile to my face. "I must have been in a real trance to have not heard that!" I laughed.

As Lilith and Loki continued their battle for dominance, I walked across the kitchen to make Gayle a cup of coffee. She smiled when I handed it to her, and I felt a pain in my chest. I couldn't help but think that my time with her might be limited. I didn't want to think this way. I didn't want the negative possibilities to take over my thoughts. They were the reality I would have to face if I made even the smallest of mistakes.

"I have some exciting news." She had a glow that I hadn't seen in her for quite a while. The light in her eyes immediately changed my train of thought.

"Let me guess! Logan has finally decided to stop acting like he isn't interested in you and actually asked you out?" I knew it was wishful thinking, but I couldn't control the urge to push her on the issue any time an opportunity presented itself.

She laughed. "No. I doubt that man will ever get over himself and do that. We'll both just keep acting like there's nothing there for the rest of eternity." There was a hint of disappointment in her expression when she said that.

"You know you could ask him out, right? Women are allowed to ask me out now. They've been doing it for years now." I handed her the cup of coffee, and we sat down at the kitchen table. The dogs had finally grown tired of their battle and came over to lay down next to us.

Gayle audibly gasped as if she was completely shocked by what I had said. The woman was nothing if she wasn't dramatic. "Nope. Not gonna happen. It would make me look desperate, and I am not desperate." There was a notable absence of humor in the statement. She genuinely believed that she would appear desperate if she asked him out on a date.

"Fine. Be stubborn." I squeezed her hand. "We won't get into this argument again, but only because I know that it's pointless. You won't change your mind. I'll just have to push him instead." I noticed a blush come across her face.

"You will do no such thing!" She sounded offended. "That won't look any less desperate than me asking him myself. Quit meddling." She reached over and pinched underneath my arm.

The pinch actually hurt a bit, but I definitely exaggerated the extent of the pain. "Ouch! I promise to let it go if you promise to stop abusing me!"

"You're such a drama queen." She actually sounded like she was scolding me.

I stood up and extended my hand toward her. "Hello, Pot. I'm Kettle. It's nice to meet you!" She glared at me before falling into a fit of laughter that shook the table. "Now that we've gotten that out of our system for the week, please tell me the news that has you so excited." I sat back down and waited for her to stop laughing.

Once she settled down, she blurted out, "Laura is pregnant again! She's due in March. She called and told me last night."

I leaned over and hugged her tightly. I knew how happy this news made her. She took no greater pride in anything other than her ability to tell people she was a grandma. "That's great! I bet they're hoping for a girl this time."

"I don't know what they're hoping for, but I would definitely love to finally have a granddaughter. Those boys just wear me out every time I see them. Girls just aren't as active as boys." She was so animated when she talked that she actually appeared to be growing tired just thinking about spending time with the boys.

Her happiness was contagious, and I found I was also getting excited about the new baby. "Yes, but what better way is there to be exhausted? Besides, I don't think you really care. You love every minute you get to spend with those boys."

"That is very true. I wish I could spend more time with them." The sadness in her voice cut me like a knife.

It occurred to me that now was the perfect time for her to go visit them. "Why don't you go see them? I'm leaving in a couple of days anyway. You could take the dogs. That would give the boys someone else to wear out other than you."

"Are you sure? I mean, don't get me wrong, I would love to go visit, but if we're both gone, who will take care of the house?" Gayle's dedication to her job was astonishing.

I couldn't stifle the laugh. "With none of us here, I don't think there's much to be taken care of. I can always call Logan and have him keep an eye on things. Or... You could call him." I knew she would balk at the suggestion, but I made it anyway. It was a fun little back and forth we had on a regular basis.

Gayle was smiling despite the fact that it was obvious she was trying to hide the happiness the mere thought of talking to Logan brought to her. She was like a school girl with a crush and it was adorable. "You think you're clever, don't you?"

"I know I'm clever, but that isn't the point." I reached over and tapped the back of her hand. "So, are you going to call him, or shall I?"

She drank the last sip of her coffee and stood up from the table. "Fine. I'll call him this afternoon. When should I tell him we'll be leaving?" She looked over and noticed that my cup was empty as well. "Are you finished, or would you like another cup?"

I handed the empty mug to her. "I guess I'm done. That was my third cup. I'll be heading out on Wednesday. You can go ahead and head out as soon as you're ready.

I could see that she was brimming over with excitement. "Okay. I'll call Laura in a few minutes to make sure she doesn't mind if I come to visit." She was bouncing around the kitchen like a child.

I couldn't help but laugh. "I don't think she's going to mind at all. I think it feels a little like a vacation for her when you're there."

"True. Would you like for me to make something for

breakfast? I could whip up some eggs and bacon if you want." Her voice had taken on a sing-song tone.

I thought about it for a moment but wasn't really in the mood to eat. "Nah. I'm just going to have some cereal and try to get some work done. I've still got a long list of things I need to get wrap up before I leave."

"All work and no play makes Jane a dull girl." She shot me a look that reminded me of my mother.

I walked over and dried the coffee mugs that she had placed in the dish drainer. "I can't help it. Maybe one day I'll decide to take it easy, but for now, it helps to fill the void."

"If you would go on a date once in a while it might give you something fun to fill that void you're always talking about." Again, she sounded like my mom.

I placed the mugs in the cabinet and turned around to face her. She was standing with her hands on her hips as if she was about to truly admonish me. "I'll go on a date when you do." The sass was heavy in my voice.

She rolled her eyes at me. "I think I'll go make that call to Logan now." She reached over and squeezed my arm. "I love you, kiddo."

"I love you too." Once again the possibility of screwing something up and losing her stabbed at my heart. As she turned to leave the kitchen I added, "Make sure to set up a dinner date with him for when you get back!"

She turned back around and flipped me off before walking out of the room. The dogs got up and followed her. Those three were the entirety of my family. After my parents had passed away last year, I had asked Gayle to move into the house with me. She had tried to argue, but my bluff about selling the house because it was too big for one person had managed to persuade her to see things my way. I would never have sold the house, but I didn't want to be in this house alone either. I knew that since her children had moved away several years earlier, it didn't make much sense for both of us to live alone when we got along so well. My parents had hired her as our housekeeper when I was barely out of diapers. She had been a fixture in my life for as far back as I could remember. I wanted her here with me, and I wasn't taking no for an answer.

FOUR

I sat in my office trying to get everything organized for my trip to Birmingham. I could feel the anxiety start to build. I had been planning this for so long, but it was just beginning to sink in that I was actually going to go through with it. I couldn't screw this up. It would mean the end of my life. Literally.

I called Mike to make sure that the documents I needed were on the way. "Well, hey, beautiful!" His voice was song-like. He was entirely too happy to talk to me.

"Hey, Mike. How's it going?" I despised small talk, especially when it was over the phone.

"Fast and furious, as usual. I have a never-ending supply of spoiled trust fund kids willing to spend way too much money on fake IDs. I may even be able to retire before I hit forty." It always amazed me how much pleasure he got from his work. I wanted that kind of passion and joy in my life.

I was smiling, and it could be heard in my voice. "Are you calling me spoiled?" I knew that he wasn't, but I always took any opportunity presented to me to make him squirm.

"Of course not! You are a trust fund kid, though, so if the shoe fits..." He chuckled, and I couldn't help but laugh silently myself.

I quickly composed myself, trying my best to sound serious. "I never asked for the trust fund. I'm not complaining about having it, mind you, but it wasn't something I ever wanted or expected."

"No, I suppose you didn't. I don't think you would have needed it if your parents hadn't set it up for you. You're probably the smartest person I know, and nothing keeps you from accomplishing the things you set out to do." I could tell he meant what he had just said. He was always complimenting me, but they were genuine compliments. "I guess you're calling to see if your things are ready. I sent them out yesterday. You should have them by this afternoon." He changed the subject because he knew that I would quickly steer him away from a conversation that revolved around how great I was.

"Thank you. You don't know how much I appreciate you getting them done so quickly. I can pay you extra if you want. You know I can just sleep on a smaller pile of money tonight. I won't miss it." Sarcasm is my second language, and I speak it fluently.

"You could always show your appreciation by letting me take you out to dinner when you get back from whatever goodwill mission you are heading out on this time." He never let a conversation come to an end without asking me out on a date.

It made me uncomfortable every time. It wasn't because I

didn't want to go out with him. I did. I do. I just didn't know that it was a smart move, and it violated my rule about mixing business relationships with personal ones. "I'll think about it, but I can't make any promises."

"Do you ever make promises?" I swear I could hear his eyes roll as he said it. I definitely heard him sigh out of frustration.

"No." I hated being this way towards him.

"Is there a specific reason for that? Is it a policy that you have for everyone, or just for me?" As much as I didn't want to have this conversation either, I was glad he wasn't still pushing me to go out with him.

"It's an across the board policy. Promises should never be broken, and there's never any guarantee that I'll be able to keep them. Therefore, I just don't make them at all." It was the truth. My parents had drilled it into me as a child to not make promises I couldn't keep. I simply took it one step further by never making any at all.

He laughed. "Don't you ever get tired of being so damn honest about everything?"

"Honest? I don't think honesty is one of my better personality traits. You did just make me yet another fake ID. That's not exactly something an honest person has a need for on a regular basis." If he knew how dishonest I actually was, he would probably stop talking to me altogether.

There was a full-on roar of laughter on the other end of the line. "That's different, and you know it. You do that so that you don't bring attention to yourself for all the good deeds you do. It's probably one of the most respectable things about you. A true, selfless humanitarian, that's what you are."

He paused, and I could hear him take a drag from a cigarette. "You try to play it off like you aren't anyone special, but you are actively working to make the world a better place, and you refuse to take any credit for it. I guess I can see why you refuse to go out with me. We are completely different people. You are out improving people's lives, and I'm making it possible for underage brats to get drunk."

I couldn't help but laugh. He was wrong about so many things, but I couldn't tell him that. "Ah, but you redeem yourself by helping me. You help me, so you are also helping to make the world a better place. It balances out in the end."

"If you say so. I don't do it for free, so there's that little hitch." I started to feel bad for him. He sounded disappointed in himself.

I changed my tone and tried to sound positive. "You don't charge me as much as you do them, so it's okay. Besides, what kind of businessman would you be if you gave away your products for free?"

"Why does it not surprise me that you would look at it that way? Always looking for the positive in any situation." He sounded less pessimistic.

I had to keep the conversation going in this direction. "There's always a positive side to everything. You just have to take the time to look for it."

"Whatever you say, Miss Congeniality." He was mocking me again.

He had come back around, and I took the opportunity to end the conversation on the high note. "Okay. I've got to get back to work. I'll text you as soon as I receive the package. Thank you again."

One of the best things about Mike was that he never tried to drag out a conversation for no reason. "No problem. Call me when you get back from wherever you're going this time."

"I will. Later asshole!" We always ended our conversations the same way.

"Later goody-two-shoes!" He hung up, and the line went silent.

As I laid my phone down on my desk, I thought about how much I actually liked Mike. He really was a genuinely good guy despite his shady business dealings. If I felt like I had the time to have a real relationship with someone I would probably choose him. We have known each other for several years, introduced by a mutual friend when I was in college. I found it a bit ironic that I met him when I was nineteen but never bought a fake ID from him until after I had turned twenty-one. I guess I had earned the "goody-two-shoes" nickname. I never had a single drink of alcohol until after my twenty-first birthday. I had also never taken any drugs that weren't prescribed to me. Thinking about it now, I realized that to everyone else I must seem like such a bore. If they only knew.

I pulled the file folder out of the bottom drawer of my desk. I would need to burn all of it before I left. I couldn't risk anyone ever knowing that I was connected to Daniel Poppock in even the smallest of ways. I was going to destroy the laptop that I had used to do all of the research on him as well. After everything was said and done, there would be no way anyone could find anything that could connect me to him. It would all be in my head.

He deserved everything that was coming to him and probably a great deal more. According to the court documents, he had ordered the deaths of five people, three of them children, because the father owed him money related to some botched drug deal. The person who had carried out the order had been caught because he was stupid enough to get hurt while taking their lives and had left plenty of DNA evidence at the scene. As soon as he was arrested, he turned on Poppock to avoid the death penalty.

Of course, Poppock was arrested, and his trial had been swift. He had been found guilty after the jury deliberated for only twenty minutes. He was sentenced to death. The justice system had worked, or so it had seemed at the time.

Two weeks after his sentence was handed down it was discovered that the person responsible for conducting the DNA testing had been altering results. She had been dating a detective and would make sure that the results came out the way he wanted them to. Multiple cases came under review, including the case of the man that had pulled the trigger on Poppock's orders. The DNA results in his case were thrown out, and he was released until a new trial could be held.

The bigger problem came when it was realized that the original blood samples had been compromised and could not be tested further. The other guy recanted his statement and claimed that he had never had anything to do with any of it and that he had only agreed to confess and point the finger at Poppock when police had told him he would be put to death if he didn't give them the information they wanted. The entire thing was a disaster that ended with both men being set free and not much chance of either man being re-tried

The triggerman had been found dead in a hotel room one month after his release. He had overdosed on heroin. Poppock had quietly moved out of his old neighborhood, and most people had no idea where he had gone. I imagined that he has started to feel like he didn't run much risk of being found out at this point. I intended to shatter that sense of security.

A knock on my office door startled me back into reality. Gayle opened the door just enough to stick her head in. "Hey, sweetie. This package just came for you." She held a brown envelope in her hand.

"Oh, thank you, Gayle." I stood up from my chair and walked over to her to get the package. "I've been waiting for this. Have you had a chance to call Logan and Laura?"

She leaned against the door frame. "Yes. Logan said he would keep an eye on things while we're gone. Laura and the boys are excited that I'm coming. Actually, I think the boys are more excited that I'm bringing the dogs. You know Jason won't let them have any pets, so this is a real treat for them. I'll be leaving in the morning if that's okay with you."

My heart sank. Tonight could be my last night with her. I had to do this right. If I screwed up and got caught, it would kill her. "That's fine. Can we have dinner tonight?"

"I've already got it working!" She stood up straight as if she was proud of having already thought of dinner. "I figured you wouldn't mind meatloaf."

The woman knew me all too well. "Of course not. It's the best thing you make." It may sound odd, but her meatloaf truly was amazing.

"I will never understand you, child. I can cook any meal

as well as any trained chef, yet you swoon over meatloaf. You're weird." She was shaking her head.

I grabbed her arm and squeezed. "I don't like everyone's meatloaf, just yours. Besides, me being weird is one of the things you love most about me."

"It is one of your more endearing qualities." She reached up and pinched my earlobe. I didn't know when or why it started, but it was something she did often when she was feeling sentimental. "Anyway, dinner will be ready in about an hour."

"Why so early?" We always ate later than we should. "Are you leaving so early that you need to go to bed before the sun even goes down?"

She laughed. "It's not early, dear. It's already almost seven."

"Really? I guess I've just been so consumed with this project that I completely lost track of time." I had no idea it had gotten so late. I had been in my own little world for hours.

She rolled her eyes at me. "That's not unusual. Not for you anyway."

"True." I couldn't argue with her about it. I definitely had a tendency to become consumed with things and lose all track of time. "By the way, I'm going to transfer some money into your account for your trip. Don't even try to argue. Feeding those two mutts of mine isn't cheap, and I don't want you spending your money on them. I'm going to give you some extra so that you can spoil the boys too."

Her face lit up and she was grinning ear to ear. "Laura won't like that."

"Like you care." I knew one of her favorite things to do

was spoil her grandkids.

She stepped back out of the room. "I definitely don't." She started walking down the hall, and I could hear her humming as she got further away.

I walked back to my desk and opened the package from Mike. The IDs were perfect; not that I expected anything less. Mike could fool the secret service, his work was so good. As I looked at them, I realized the name he had put on them. I picked up my phone and sent him a message.

"Charity Hilton? Really?"

"I thought it was perfect lol"

"Asshole"

"Goody two shoes"

"Later"

After washing the dishes I took the dogs out to the backyard for one final romp before I headed to bed myself. I sat in the lounge chair and watched Lilith and Loki play. I thought back to how they had come into my life. Lilith had been a gift from Gayle. She had rescued her from a shelter after my parents died. She came into my bedroom one afternoon and begged me not to be mad at her. It was at that point that I noticed the leash hanging from her hand. As soon as I saw Lilith, I fell in love. She was absolutely beautiful. She is mostly pit bull but one hundred percent gentle giant. Her markings are brown and white like a cow and her eyes are a beautiful golden color. It was obvious from the very start that she had never been shown any real affection. It had taken several months for her to come out of her shell. Now, she is one of the most affectionate dogs you could ever dream of meeting.

Loki had been a gift as well. From Lilith. I would never forget that morning. I had been working on deep cleaning the kitchen, against Gayle's objections, and Lilith had been pacing back and forth at the door for several minutes, despite having only been back inside for a short time. I finally let her back out, basically because she was getting on my nerves. It was a nice day, so I just left the door open. Because my house is off the beaten path, I don't have a fenced yard, but Lilith had never gone very far. She came back in just a few minutes later. I had my head in one of the lower cabinets scrubbing away months of dust and general nastiness. I heard a whimper and bumped my head on the cabinet when I turned around. Lilith was standing there with a grin on her face and a dirty puppy at her feet. I don't know where she found him, but she had decided that he was hers. I took him to the vet that day. I didn't get a chance to finish cleaning the kitchen. Gayle had that task completed by the time I got home with a completely healthy German Shepherd mix puppy. That day, my family felt complete again for the first time in a long time.

I let the two of them run and play until they had no energy left. We walked back inside, and they both immediately jumped on the living room couch and curled up to go to sleep. It was just one more moment today that reminded me that I couldn't make any mistakes. I would miss this if I lost it. I had to do this right. I had to come back to my family with full confidence that our lives wouldn't be disrupted because of my stupid desire to make things right.

I double checked all of the locks and set the alarm before I headed upstairs to my bedroom. I took a quick shower and swallowed a muscle relaxer before crawling into bed. Sleep didn't come easily. I couldn't stop going over every detail of my plan. Even the muscle relaxer wasn't helping to ease the tension in my body.

FIVE

I despise alarm clocks! When mine started going off at five a.m. I cursed the day and my life. I didn't want to get up. I crawled out of my bed and immediately headed to the shower. I was in desperate need of overly-hot water, as every muscle in my body was tense and knotted. I tried to convince myself that all of this would be over and done with next week. By then the entire reason I had been feeling so stressed would be in the past. The deed would be done, and I would be able to move on. Despite what I told myself, it didn't help to calm me down.

As much as I hated the thought of it, I decided that I may need to take the anti-anxiety medication that my therapist had prescribed for me.

I stepped out of the shower, feeling only slightly better. I opened the medicine cabinet and stared at the pill bottle. After some internal debate, I decided against taking one now. I needed to be clear in my thoughts. I would have to find some other way to get over this feeling. I headed back into my bedroom and immediately turned back around to look at the medicine cabinet again. I realized that those little pills might actually prove to be useful. I grabbed the bottle and placed it in the bag that I had begun to pack a couple of days ago. As I reached the bottom of the staircase, I saw Gayle's bags sitting by the front door. Once again, a sinking feeling of fear rushed over me. This was going to be much harder than I had anticipated. I felt my breathing start to get heavy, and my heart began to race. I was losing my cool. I needed Gayle. I needed her now. "Gayle! Where are you?" I shouted across the house.

"I'm right here, dear. Why did you sound so panicked?" Gayle came strolling out of the kitchen with a worried look on her face.

The mere sight of her calmed me down. I would never make it through this life without her. "No reason. I guess I'm just a bit on edge this morning. I don't really know why." I hated lying to her.

"Everything is going to be fine. You do this every time you go out of town. Maybe you don't realize it, but you do. If you would just let people know that it's you instead of trying to hide your good deeds, you wouldn't be so stressed out." She was smiling at me in a way that made me think of my mother.

I sighed. "You know I can't do that. It's not truly a good deed if you're looking for a pat on the back for having done it."

"You sound like your mother. Letting people know you did it doesn't mean you are looking for a pat on the back. I understand that you don't want to be praised, but is it worth the secrecy if it causes you such mental anguish?" She had a point, but I wasn't going to let her know that.

The dogs had joined us by this point, and they were both nipping at my feet. "I'd have it either way. Six of one, half a dozen of the other."

"Have it your way, then." She shook her head and rolled her eyes. She was the queen of the eye roll. "I'll be here for you either way. Except for the next few days, of course! Thank you so much for letting me go see the kids. I've really missed them."

I shooed the dogs away and gave her a hug. "You know you don't have to wait for me to tell you to go, but we won't get into that debate again today. Save it for another time." I stepped back and looked at her bags sitting by the door. "Have you got everything together already? Can I help you with anything?"

"It's all done. I've actually just been waiting for you to come down. Unlike some people in this house, I didn't spend half the day in bed." She laughed.

The dogs had come back and were desperately trying to get our attention. It was obvious they knew they were about to go somewhere. They absolutely loved going for rides in the car. "My apologies. Next time I'll set my alarm for four."

"Well, then you'd only be an hour behind me!" She pinched my earlobe again. "If you don't mind, I'd like to go ahead and leave now. I don't want to get caught up in morning traffic."

I reached down and picked up one of her bags. It was heavier than I had expected it to be. "That's fine. Let me help you load these bags into the car."

We carried the bags to her car, and the dogs came bouncing behind us. I spent several minutes petting and hugging them before they happily jumped into her back seat. I turned to Gayle to hug her. She could see the tears that were beginning to flood my eyes.

"Why are you crying? It's only a week!" She wiped a tear from my cheek.

I took her hand in mine. "I know, but I do actually miss you when you aren't around."

"You won't even notice. You've got plenty to do to keep yourself occupied. If you didn't, you wouldn't have suggested that I leave in the first place. I love you, sweetheart. I'll call you as soon as I get to Laura's house. I should be there around two." She walked over and closed the trunk of her car.

I was frozen. I couldn't make myself move. This really hurt. "Okay. I love you! Drive carefully, and call me if there are any delays." I was choking on my words.

"I will. I love you too!" She hugged me, and I didn't want to let go. I wanted her to stay. I didn't want to go through with this any longer.

It felt like a final goodbye. I didn't think it was possible, but my heart sank even further. How was I supposed to make it through this? I must be completely insane to believe that I can accomplish this and come out of it without consequences. There are always consequences, and this time they were going to be bad.

I stood in silence as I watched her car turn out of the driveway. Wiping away tears, I headed back into the house. Stepping into the living room, I felt utterly alone. I didn't know what I was supposed to do. I had so much to get done today, but no desire to do any of it at the moment.

I spent the next hour getting everything I needed to be packed into one bag. I laughed to myself about how little I was taking with me. Only the absolute necessities. I would buy most of what I needed on the way to Birmingham. This was the routine. I couldn't stray from the routine. It kept me safe. It kept me anonymous. That was more important now than it had ever been before. KISS. Keep It Simple Stupid.

I headed to my office to go back over the Poppock file one last time. Once again, I became so absorbed in the material that I lost track of time. The ringing of my phone startled me back to reality. I didn't have to look at the caller ID to know that it was Gayle. The ringtone I had set for her was the song that she was always whistling while she cleaned. It brought an immediate smile to my face. "Hey, Gayle! Have you made it to Laura's?"

"Yes, dear. I'm sitting outside right now watching the boys play with the dogs. At the rate they're going, I doubt any of them will make it more than an hour past dinner before passing out from exhaustion!" Even if she hadn't been laughing, I would have been able to tell that she was happier than she had been in a long time.

"I'm glad you've made it safely and that you seem to be having a good time. Make sure you relax while you're there. Remember, this is a vacation for you. You aren't Laura's maid. You're mine." I knew the reminder was pointless but decided to throw it out there anyway.

She laughed. "I know, but you know I can't help myself sometimes. I actually enjoy cleaning." It was definitely true. I had once caught her cleaning the vacuum. It was the most ridiculous thing I had ever seen.

"I know that you do. Now, stop talking to me and enjoy your time with those kids! Call me if you need me, though." I knew she would stay on the phone all afternoon giving me a play by play of what was going on if I didn't end the call myself.

"What time are you leaving tomorrow, and when do you plan to be back?" Gayle was always keeping tabs on me.

I thought about it for a moment before answering her. My plans were well thought out, but I knew that even small obstacles could throw things off. "I'm leaving early tomorrow morning. I should be back no later than next Wednesday, but it'll probably be late."

"Alright. Stay safe. You call me if anything changes." I could tell that she was distracted. I heard a child scream in the background. "I've got to go. These four don't know how to play nicely."

I couldn't help but laugh. "Okay. Go play referee. I love you."

"I love you too. Text me when you leave in the morning." She hung up the phone before I could say anything else. I wondered who had been crying and who had caused it. I hoped it wasn't one of the dogs hurting one of the kids. I wouldn't be able to forgive myself if that was the case.

I headed back to my office and sat down at my desk, and I started reviewing the facts again.

Once I was satisfied that I had it all down, I took the file out to the backyard and threw it in the fire pit. I lit the fire and settled into my lounge chair. As I watched the fire burn, I could see each individual article and piece of information clearly in my mind. My confidence was beginning to build back up, and my anxiety settled back down. I sat and watched the fire until it burned itself out. By that time it was nearly nine o'clock. I needed to head to bed. I had to get up early in the morning.

I made my way to my bedroom and settled into bed. It seemed to take forever for me to get to sleep. I couldn't stop going over every little detail I had planned for the next several days. Once I did finally get to sleep it wasn't peaceful. My dreams were awful. Filled with violence, blood, and death. I woke up twice, sweating and in tears. The third time I woke up, I was screaming Gayle's name. I looked at the clock and saw that it wasn't even four yet. It didn't matter. I wasn't going back to sleep. It would have been pointless. I decided to just go ahead and take a shower. It was time to get this show on the road.

SIX

My first stop was at a small beauty supply store just outside of Louisville. I needed a wig. My real hair was a dark, chocolate brown that fell just below my shoulder blades. I think I may have been one of the few women on the planet that actually liked her natural hair. I had never felt the need to color it, and I was perfectly content with the slight wave that it had. I considered myself lucky because, at age twenty-three, I hadn't found even one gray hair. That may sound odd, but I remembered my mother telling me that her hair had started turning gray when she was twenty. By the time she passed away, her hair was completely gray.

I spent almost an hour looking for the perfect wig. I ended up buying two. One was the same color as my natural hair, but it was cut into a bob. The second was platinum blonde and cut in long layers. I enjoyed shopping for them more than I had anticipated and decided that I would buy more later. The thought of looking completely different without actually changing anything about myself was appealing, and it would definitely be useful in the future.

I texted Gayle before I left to let her know that I was already on the road. I told her that I would be driving for a while, so she didn't need to be concerned if I didn't answer her any time soon. I didn't stop again until I was close to Nashville. By this point, I was starving and in desperate need of some physical activity.

I grabbed a quick bite to eat, making sure not to eat too much so that I wouldn't end up in a food coma. Next, I went to Wal-Mart. I bought a prepaid cell phone, some new clothes, and the basic toiletries that I would need during my time in Birmingham. I stopped at a gas station and got possibly the worst cup of coffee ever brewed. I didn't care. I needed the caffeine. I had to get the last leg of this drive behind me. I had just under three hours left to drive. I was ready for it to be over. I was ready for all of this to be over.

Once I arrived in Birmingham, I drove straight to the airport. I parked my car in long-term parking before catching a cab to my chosen motel. The River Run Inn was nothing to look at inside or out. It was as basic as you could get. My room was cleaner than I had expected, but it didn't keep me from spraying down the bed with disinfectant before sitting on it. Everything in the room was at least ten years out of date. The television was the old, box style type, and the maroon carpet was worn and faded. There was no micro-fridge, so I would definitely be eating out while I was here. If everything went according to plan, I would be leaving in four days. I was ready to go now. I didn't really want to be here, but my determination to see this through was stronger than my desire to be comfortable at home.

I walked across the street to the small diner I had noticed when I arrived. They seemed reasonably busy for this time of night, which was a good thing. The more customers they had, the easier it would be for me to go unnoticed. I wasn't overly hungry, so I only ordered a grilled cheese sandwich and fries. As I ate I watched the other customers. There was a younger couple cuddled up in a booth in the corner. They were giggling and a bit too touchy-feely for my comfort. I wondered how much alcohol had been consumed between the two of them. I doubted either of them were even old enough to legally drink.

An older gentleman was sitting at the bar across from the grill. The lone waitress spent most of her free time talking to him. He was probably in his late sixties, and I imagined that being here was part of his nightly routine. The tow of them talked about how their respective days had been. He told her about his doctor's appointment earlier, where he had nearly passed out having an ingrown toenail removed. I silently chuckled at how dramatic and animated he was in his description of the whole ordeal. It wasn't an appropriate conversation to be having while people were trying to eat. I was grateful for an iron stomach.

The waitress complained about how she and her husband had gotten into yet another giant argument this morning. Apparently, she had caught him talking to another woman online, and he believed she was making too big of a deal out of it. I had to resist the urge to tell her to trust her instincts. Even with my limited life experience, I knew that a woman's intuition is usually right. Sadly, all too often we tried to talk ourselves out of believing what was blatantly obvious to the rest of the world.

I finished eating but continued to eavesdrop on their conversation until my eyelids began to feel heavy. I left the money for my food and tip on the table. On the back of the bill I scribbled "trust your gut." I walked back across the street to my disappointing accommodations. I changed into the new pajamas I had bought and crawled under the sheets. I closed my eyes and tried not to think about the very real possibility that I was going to be a buffet for a family of bed bugs. It didn't take long for me to drift off into a fitful sleep.

I woke up the next morning around ten I looked online to find a restaurant within walking distance of Poppock's house. I called a cab to pick me up before changing into appropriate clothes for walking. I also put on the short brown wig. I had to look different if I was going to walk around *his* neighborhood. I hoped that the new shoes I was wearing wouldn't become uncomfortable or rub blisters on my heels today.

The cabbie drove me to the Chinese restaurant I had decided on. While I ate, I downloaded and set up a music streaming app on the phone I had bought yesterday. I had left mine back at the motel. I didn't want to somehow get caught walking around with two phones. I had also left my real IDs. Today, I was Charity Hilton.

I finished my meal and headed outside. I popped my headphones in my ears and turned on the classic rock station I had found. I familiarized myself with my surroundings and headed out, walking in the general direction of Poppock's house. I had memorized all of the different roads in the area quite a while back. I casually strolled through the neighborhood, noticing that he had somehow managed to find himself a place to live in a relatively well-off area. I didn't have to guess what he was doing to have the income to be able to afford living here.

When I made the turn onto the street where he lived, I took note of the house numbers. I was three blocks away from his house. All of the houses had the same basic design. The vast majority were brick, split-level homes with attached garages. As I approached Poppock's house, I saw that it didn't stand out from the others as I had assumed it would. I supposed I had presumed that there would be something about his that would look different. One day I would learn to dismiss the preconceived notions surrounding certain types of people. I had pictured the drug dealer living in the most run-down house on the block, with attack dogs in the yard. He had successfully squashed that stereotype for me.

Three laps through the neighborhood left me feeling confident that I had all the information that I needed to successfully get in and out of his house without any issues. I had been able to determine the general layout of the house. I didn't really need details. There were only three entrances to the house, and I had already decided that the door in the backyard was going to be the easiest point of entry. Luckily, I didn't see any visible sign of him owning dogs. As a matter of fact, there were surprisingly few in the entire neighborhood.

I didn't know why, but I decided to make one last pass by his house. I turned the corner back onto his block and instantly regretted it. He was standing in his driveway, leaned into the driver's window of the car that was now parked there. I pushed back the urge to turn around. Sudden movements get you noticed. I was on the same side of the street as his house and only two houses away. There was no way he wasn't going to see me. I tried to maintain a leisurely stride and not look nervous. As I got closer, I saw him look in my direction. He said something to the man in the car and started walking in my direction. Dammit! This was the last thing I needed. The car pulled out of his driveway, and he stood there smiling at me, waiting for me to get closer.

He had a creepy grin on his face. "It's a beautiful day for a walk," he chirped. His voice wasn't at all what I expected.

"Yes, it is," I said without even slowing my pace.

He started walking next to me, and I hoped that he wouldn't want to wander too far from his house. "I don't think I've ever seen you before. New to the neighborhood?"

This was pathetic. If I hadn't known who he was, I would have almost felt bad for him. "Yeah. I just moved here a couple of weeks ago. I'm just now getting a chance to get out to get a feel for the neighborhood."

We reached the end of the block. He stopped walking. I didn't. "Don't be a stranger, new neighbor! My name's Danny. Feel free to let me know if you need anything." The emphasis he put on the word anything made the implication clear.

As I reached the other side of the street, I turned and nodded in his direction so that he knew that I had heard him. I wanted to be out of there so badly that I almost broke into a run. Twenty minutes later I was back at the strip mall where the Chinese restaurant was located. I called another cab to take me back to my motel.

I had been beating myself up about the decision to walk by his house one last time but had eventually decided that it probably wasn't the worst thing that could have happened. His size was no longer just numbers on a piece of paper. I had been able to really size him up. He wasn't much taller than me. He definitely wasn't in better shape than me. He probably outweighed me by fifty pounds or so, but that would be easily overcome. I stopped by the motel office and asked if there was a decent bar in the area. The older woman working at the front desk directed me to a hole-in-the-wall place just two blocks over.

Had the clerk at the desk not described the place to me, I would never have noticed it. The windows were so filthy that I could barely tell that there were lights on inside. This was actually kinda perfect. No name bars like this are exactly what a person in my position needed. No one asks or cares why you are there.

SEVEN

It felt as if his eyes had pierced my soul. He looked like the poster boy for a reality television dating show. He was wearing jeans and a polo, and his hair was perfect. His physique indicated that he worked out, but he wasn't bulky. I wondered what someone like him was doing in a bar like this. He was so well put together compared to the other patrons. Everyone else looked like they had been worn down by life. As that thought crossed my mind, I realized that I probably stood out as well. Coming here had obviously been a bad decision, but I realized it would seem odd if I turned around and left at this point. I walked up to the bar and took a seat three stools down from Mr. Distraction.

I was making a decidedly concentrated effort to avoid making further eye contact, despite my desire to simply sit and stare at him. I ordered a bourbon neat and noticed that the bartender didn't flinch at my order. I didn't drink often and went to bars even less frequently, but I'd noticed that bartenders usually look at me like I've got a third eye in the middle of my forehead when I placed my order. I guess I didn't fit the profile of someone who appreciated good bourbon.

"That'll be seven dollars." The bartender placed my drink on a napkin in front of me.

I handed him ten dollars and nodded. "Keep the change."

"Thank you, ma'am. Let me know if you need anything else." I had forgotten how southerners seem to call everyone sir or ma'am.

I looked up at the television over the bar. There was a college basketball game on, and I pretended to be interested in the game instead of in the man that was sitting less than ten feet away from me. I was struggling against the urge to look in his direction. It was like I was being pulled in his direction by gravity. This was not how I had imagined this night going. I definitely didn't need to complicate this trip any further, but I was almost certain at this point that I wasn't going to be able to resist the temptation.

Raised voices across the room grabbed my attention. There were two rather large gentlemen arguing at the pool table in the corner. My momentary concern that a fight would actually break out was diminished when I realized they were simply arguing about whose turn it was to pay for the next game.

"They do that every night. I think they just genuinely like to argue with one another." It took a moment for me to recognize that the bartender was speaking to me.

I took a drink and felt the warmth of the bourbon run down my throat. "I was worried for a minute there."

"No need to worry. We don't see much trouble here. The

biggest problem we ever really see is folks getting upset when I insist they take a cab home." He was wiping the bar top down with a towel that was probably spreading more germs than it was killing.

I was absentmindedly running my finger along the edge of my glass. "No one likes to hear that they've had too much to drink."

"True. Are you about ready for another?" He grinned, and I was thrown off by how perfect his teeth were. I wondered if they were dentures. They didn't seem to go with the somewhat scruffy appearance he presented.

I glanced down at my almost empty glass. "I suppose one more won't hurt. I'm not trying to get wasted. Just need to take the edge off this day."

"I don't know many people who drink bourbon to get wasted." He poured me a fresh drink and replaced my empty glass with the new one. "This one's on Chris." He nodded toward Mr. Distraction.

I refused to look at him, choosing instead to look straight down at the bar top. "Tell him I said thanks."

"You can tell him yourself. He's harmless, and I ain't no messenger service." He laughed and turned to walk away.

I took a deep breath before standing up. I knew this was the first in a line of huge mistakes I would be making tonight. I picked up my drink and purse and moved to the seat next to Chris. "Thank you for the drink."

He didn't turn to look at me, and I wondered if I had been wrong about the entire situation. "You're welcome. I don't often buy drinks for strangers, but I don't often see a beautiful woman ordering good bourbon either."

"Well, I don't usually accept drinks from strangers, but apparently today is the type of day where I do a lot of things I wouldn't normally do." I could feel myself beginning to blush. This was completely out of character for me.

He finally turned his gaze my direction and raised his eyebrows. "Oh really? Like what?" He was obviously extremely interested in what my answer to this question was going to be. It was exactly the motivation that I needed to be as bold as I wanted to be.

"Like, I'm really hoping that we can finish up these drinks and go find a hotel room." I couldn't believe how easily the words fell out of my mouth.

He took his wallet out and laid a twenty dollar bill down on the bar. "I'd have to be crazy to turn down a proposition like that. Do you have a specific hotel in mind?"

"Nope. I'm not from here. I don't have a clue what hotels are close by. As long as I don't have to worry about bedbugs, I'm good. You pick. I'll pay." I downed the remainder of my drink.

He stood up and motioned toward the door. As we started to walk away, he shouted back to the bartender, "Greg, we're leaving. Money's on the bar."

We walked outside, and he said his car was around the corner. I wondered if I had lost my mind because nothing about this scared me at all. I was leaving a bar with a man I had only met minutes earlier. He hadn't even asked my name. I was actually amused at how reckless I was being in this moment. It was an adrenaline rush, and I was consumed by the excitement of it all.

We got to his car, and for some reason, it surprised me

that he opened the door for me. As we pulled away, he started laughing. "This is funny to you?" I asked.

"Yes, actually. I'm thirty-two years old, and this is the first time I have ever picked up some random woman in a bar. I wasn't even trying to either." He seemed strangely proud of himself.

I turned sideways in my seat so that I could look at him directly. He was wonderful to look at. "This wasn't exactly my plan either."

"Good to know." He didn't sound like he believed me. "If it had been your plan, I wouldn't judge you for it. We all have our needs."

I was trying to decide if I should be offended or not when his words struck me. "Hey, ummm. Speaking of needs... unless you have some protection on you, we are going to need to make a pit stop before we get to whatever hotel you're taking me to."

"Pit stop it is. I'm fairly certain that there's a gas station next door to the hotel." We were both silent for a couple of minutes before he blurted out, "I must seem like a complete ass! I haven't even asked you what your name is."

"Charity." I couldn't help but laugh at how ridiculous it sounded for me to claim that was my name.

He turned into a gas station and parked the car. "Well, Charity, I'm gonna run in here real quick. Is there anything else I should add to the shopping list?"

"Nothing I can think of at the moment." I really only wanted him to hurry up before I lost my nerve.

"Okay, I'll be right back. I won't hold it against you if you take this opportunity to run." He smiled, and I noticed that his teeth were perfect. I imagined that his parents had paid a pretty penny when he was younger for him to have that perfect smile.

"I'm not going to run," I said it, but internally I was considering doing exactly that.

He leaned into the car and kissed me. It was as if he was begging me with a kiss to not leave. "If you change your mind, this is a safe neighborhood. There's a Waffle House down the street where you could wait for a cab."

"Would you just hurry up?" I practically screamed at him. That kiss had melted my insides it had been so hot.

"Yes, ma'am!" He shut the door to the car and practically ran into the store. I sat laughing the entire time he was inside. I looked around trying to figure out what hotel he had chosen. There was a Hilton within sight, and I hoped that was where we were headed.

He returned to the car still smiling. "I'm so glad you didn't run."

"I told you I wouldn't." I was ready to rip his clothes off.

He got back in the car and started the engine. "Is the Hilton okay? I'm paying. Don't argue. I wouldn't be able to continue to call myself a gentleman if I let you pay." He was already backing out of the parking spot.

"The Hilton is perfect, but I really don't mind paying." I was actually a bit relieved that he offered to pay because I didn't have a credit card on me, and the high-end hotels looked at you like you're from another planet if you try to pay with cash.

"Nope. I can't let you do it." He sounded offended.

We were back on the main road. I reached over and

squeezed his upper thigh. "Fine, but you aren't allowed to say no to anything else for the rest of the night."

"Good God, woman! Don't say anything else until we get to our room, otherwise, I may not be able to make it to the room!" There was an excitement in his voice that made me want him even more.

I motioned as if I was locking my lips and smiled. It took less than a minute for us to make it to the parking lot of the Hilton. I waited for him to open my door for me. He grabbed my hand and practically dragged me into the lobby. I sat down and quietly waited while he paid for a room. He turned around a couple of minutes later and flashed a smile and a room key in my direction. I got up and followed him to the elevator. I maintained my silence until we were in the elevator and he pressed the button for the eleventh floor.

We were the only ones on the elevator, and as the doors closed, I shot a look at him that didn't require any explanation. "May I speak now?" I asked.

He immediately grabbed me and pushed me up against the back of the elevator. His hands were holding the sides of my head as his fingers were tightly grasping my hair. His lips were pressed hard against mine, and I felt as if I needed him more now than I had ever needed anything in my life. I shoved my hands up his shirt, forcing him to pull away from me briefly as I pulled it over his head. His chest was perfect. It reminded me of a professional swimmer, tight and toned without the bulk. I leaned into him and bit his lower lip. He groaned and reached down, grabbing my ass. He lifted me up, and I wrapped my legs around his waist. His mouth was now on my neck, and though I didn't think it was possible, his hot breath on my skin pushed my desire for him even higher.

We were so caught up in the moment that we didn't hear the signal that the elevator had stopped. It wasn't until we heard someone gasp that we broke away from one another. I looked up to see the shocked face of a middle-aged woman. She laughed and said, "I'll just wait for the next one."

The doors closed again, and we were right back at it. We were all over each other. Our hands and mouths didn't stop moving until the elevator did. This time we noticed when the doors opened on our floor. We practically ran to our room and barely had the door closed before we were stripping one another of our respective clothes. We didn't bother to even look around the room. We were quickly on the floor, rolling around like a couple of wild animals.

When we finally came up for air, I looked at the clock to see that it was almost one in the morning. I had no idea what time we had gotten to the hotel, but I did know that we had been here for quite a while. He got up off the floor and headed toward the bathroom. I noticed the scratches on his back. "I hope you aren't married because if you are, you're going to be in a lot of trouble."

"Definitely not married. Are you?" His tone implied that he didn't actually care about the answer to the question.

I rolled over on my stomach and looked at his naked body in its entirety. It was glorious. "No. I guess it might have been smart to have had this conversation earlier, though."

"Probably. Sometimes you have to throw caution to the wind and just live in the moment, though." He was so casual it was refreshing. I wished that I could be so nonchalant about things. Sometimes I wondered if I was ever going to actually shit out the diamond that people claimed would be coming out of my ass. I heard him turn on the shower. "I'm gonna jump in here real quick. Wanna join me?"

"Nah. I'm good. I'll wait until you get done." I was admittedly a bit sad that I was going to have to stop looking at him for a few minutes.

He stepped into the shower, leaving the bathroom door open. I was still sitting on the floor. Honestly, I was a bit concerned about the stability of my legs. I sat for a moment longer thinking about how much I had enjoyed this little escapade. Once I felt steady enough, I stood up and walked over to the bed. I contemplated putting my clothes back on and making a run for it now but decided against that plan. The bed was calling my name. It was huge, and the bedding was practically begging me to curl up in it. I grabbed the remote for the television and pulled the blankets down on the bed. I crawled in and was convinced that it would be next to impossible to get back out without being forced to do so.

Chris came out of the bathroom a few minutes later, still wet and wrapped in a towel at the waist. I looked him up and down and hoped that he would come over to ravage my body again. He noticed the look on my face and laughed. "Damn, Charity! Are you always like this?"

"Not even close. This is very out of character for me. It's been months since the last time I had sex. I'm reconsidering that lifestyle choice at the moment." I sat up on my knees facing him.

He walked toward the bed, and I felt my insides melt from the heat that was building back up inside of me. "With that kind of dry spell, you may want to consider pacing yourself." He was standing at the end of the bed at this point, looking up and down my still naked body as if I was a meal set out for a starving man.

I crawled toward him. "There's no chance in hell that I'm slowing down right now. I've still got a lot of pent-up frustration that I intend to take out on you." I snatched the towel from around his waist and pulled him down on top of me.

The next time I looked, it was three o'clock. Chris was lightly snoring next to me, and I decided to take my turn in the shower. I got up as quietly as I could. I didn't want to disturb him. I needed him to rest up. I was hoping for round three before I left in the morning.

After the most relaxing shower I had taken in weeks, I crawled back into bed. I was ready to sleep and was just on the verge of unconsciousness when I had a revelation. I had to change my plan. I didn't want to. It went against my better judgment, but I knew that I had to. The plan hadn't been right from the beginning. I simply hadn't realized it until now. I had a better idea on how to go about taking care of Poppock. It was actually quite brilliant, and I was pleased with myself for having thought of it. Perhaps this night with Chris was exactly what I needed to clear my head and be able to think straight.

EIGHT

I woke up around nine when I felt Chris start to stretch next to me in the bed. I got up and started gathering my clothes from the floor. I had wanted to have him one more time before I left, but that just wasn't going to be possible now. The change in my plan was going to require some time to work out. I didn't really have time to spare.

"You mean to tell me you aren't going to start my day off the way you finished my night?" He was looking at me with puppy-dog eyes. It was hard to resist.

"No time. I've got a lot to do today." Oh, how I wished that weren't true.

He stood up and pulled on his underwear. I wished he were still naked. Will you at least let me call you a cab?"

"That would be great. Thank you." He called a cab for me while I tried to pull myself together in the bathroom. It didn't really work, though. No matter how hard I tried, I still looked like I had been through a wild night.

When I came back out he told me that my cab would be

here in twenty minutes. "I told them that they would be taking you back to the bar. I assume you left your car there last night."

"That's not a bad assumption." There was no need to tell him otherwise. I looked over at him and noticed that he was fidgeting. That wasn't a good sign. I wasn't sure I wanted to hear whatever was about to come out of his mouth.

"Am I allowed to ask you any questions before you leave, or do you plan to go downstairs to wait?" He didn't even look up. It was as if he was embarrassed to even ask.

I sat down on the opposite side of the bed. "I'll wait here. You can ask any questions you'd like, but I won't promise to answer them."

"Fair enough." He shrugged his shoulders. "You're not from here, are you? I don't hear anything southern in your voice."

I smiled and faked, as best as I could, a southern drawl. "No, I'm not." I couldn't keep it up. It was painful to hear myself talk that way. "I'm just in town for a few days taking care of some personal business. My turn. Why is a guy like you hanging out in a bar like that?"

"My grandfather owned it before he passed away. He left it to me when he died. I don't know the first thing about running a bar, so I sold it to a family friend. I still like hanging out there, though. I've known a lot of the people that are regulars that they're like an extension of my family." He meant it. I was beginning to think he was a truly good guy. How did I manage to run across one out in the wild like that? "What were you doing there? It doesn't seem like the type of place you would frequent."

I decided to tell him the truth. Well, partially anyway. "I was just looking for a quiet place to have a drink. I actually prefer hole-in-the-wall places like that. People tend you to leave you alone in that type of place."

"True. I hope I didn't cross any lines by buying you that drink." He was smiling again.

There was definitely something about that smile that was beginning to get to me. I didn't like that fact at all. "Not at all. I'm glad you did it. I didn't know it until it happened, but last night was exactly what I needed."

"Yeah. Me too." He was staring at me.

I was trying not to stare back. I needed to get out of this room. I needed to do it now. "Look. I'm going to head downstairs before this gets awkward, and I feel like we're getting dangerously close to that point." I had never spoken any truer words.

He stood up and walked to the desk across the room. He was still only in his underwear and I was tempted to ravage him one last time before I left. He grabbed the pen and notepad and scribbled something on the top page. He walked over to me and handed me the piece of paper. "Here's my number in case you decide you'd like to call while you're still in town. I don't have anything planned over the next few days, so don't worry about disturbing me." He leaned in and kissed me. I felt my knees go weak. "I will understand if you don't call, but I hope that you do."

I steadied myself once more and said, "I'll keep that in mind." As I walked out the door, I turned around one last time. "Thanks for last night, Mr. Distraction. It was fun."

The door shut behind me before I could hear what he

said next. Luckily, someone else was getting on the elevator at that exact moment, and I was able to catch it before the doors closed. Just as they did, I could hear him call my name down the hall.

The smile didn't leave my face until I was walking back to my run-down hotel. After a night at the Hilton, I wasn't exactly excited to be back at the fleabag inn. When I got back to my room, I immediately cranked up my music and opened up my laptop. I needed to work out the details of my new plan, and I did my best thinking with music blaring in the background.

I called a cab around noon and headed back to the same shopping center I had visited yesterday. I browsed through a couple of specialty stores until my stomach loudly reminded me that I hadn't had anything to eat today. I didn't think I could handle the same Chinese place again today, so I opted for the deli that was at the end of the strip mall. The sandwich I had was surprisingly good, and I thought that I may return here if I had the chance.

After I ate, I killed a couple of hours roaming through the remaining stores. Not being much of an impulse shopper, I didn't purchase a single thing. For a moment, I thought about buying myself a souvenir. Ultimately, I decided that it wasn't a good idea. I wouldn't be taking anything home with me as a reminder of what I was going to be doing.

I headed back toward Poppock's house around the same time I had been there yesterday. Today was different, though. I was hoping to run into him again. This time I would be friendlier. My new plan wouldn't work if I didn't have the chance to see him again, and I really needed this to work.

It was my second time approaching his house that I spotted him. He was in his backyard, cleaning his grill. I walked over to the fence and watched for a moment. He had his back to me, so he didn't know that I was spying on him. I was sizing him up again. I knew, without a doubt, that I could take him down if I needed to. I still hoped that it wouldn't come to that, but it boosted my confidence to know that I could overpower him if necessary.

"Do you know what you're doing on that thing?" I yelled across the yard at him. I laughed as he jumped at the sound of my voice.

He turned and walked toward me. "You know it girl! I'm the best at everything I do!" His bravado was repulsive.

"I'm sorry, I have a horrible memory. What did you say your name was again?" It was difficult for me to hide the disgust I felt toward him. I had never taken any acting classes, and at this moment, I was regretting that particular life decision.

"Danny, but you can call me whatever name you want." Was this the best he had? Did this really work for him? I hoped that I had successfully kept myself from rolling my eyes.

"Well, Danny, I'm Charity." I still wasn't used to saying that. I didn't think it fit me at all. I'll have to be more specific about details next time I do business with Mike. "I might need you to prove to me that you're as good on that grill as you seem to think you are."

He was standing about six inches from me at this point. The only thing keeping him that far away was the chain link fence between us. "You ain't shy, are you?"

"Nope." I definitely wasn't shy. I wanted this man to think I wanted him. Last night had given me the confidence to do this.

He was preening like a peacock. This was too easy. "Alright. How about tonight?"

"I actually have plans tonight, but I'm free tomorrow evening. Would that work?" Tonight was too soon. I needed to get everything prepared.

He wasn't going to turn me down. "Yes, ma'am. Can you be here around seven?"

There was that word again. Why did it make me feel old? "Can we make it eight instead? I have a pretty full day tomorrow."

"Whatever works for you, beautiful." He licked his lips. He actually licked his lips. The man was disgusting.

I took a deep breath to calm the nausea that had come over me. "Alright, I'll see you tomorrow at eight." I turned and started walking away.

"Hey!" He shouted in my direction. "Is there anything you don't eat?"

I was surprised that he would think to even ask. "I'm sure whatever a master chef, such as yourself, decides to cook will be wonderful. Just surprise me."

"You got it." I didn't look back to see, but I assumed that he was walking with a strut at this point.

I called for a cab while I was walking back to the shopping center. I only had to wait a couple of minutes once I made it there. All I could think about was how easy it had been to get him to invite me to dinner. The timing couldn't have been any better. I knew that my plan was going to work. It added a bounce to my step, and I felt the need to celebrate this victory. I had the cabbie wait for me once we returned to my hotel. I ran inside and grabbed a change of clothes before having the cab take me back to the Hilton for the night. I also grabbed the blonde wig. I wanted to have some real fun tonight.

I got to the Hilton and was thrilled when I was able to check into the same room that Chris and I had been in last night. I unpacked the few things I had brought with me before texting him to let him know that I hoped that he would join me for another tryst tonight. He quickly replied saying that he would love to. I got his last name so that I could leave a room key for him at the front desk and asked him to meet me in the room at eight o'clock.

It was three o'clock now which gave me plenty of time to get everything ready for the night. I called and arranged for a rental car. They said it would be thirty minutes before they could pick me up. I took that time to take a quick shower before heading downstairs.

Once I was downstairs, I stopped at the front desk to let them know that I wanted to leave a room key for Chris. I gave the clerk his name and stressed that they were not to let him know my real name. I actually made sure that she wrote Charity Hilton on the envelope with the room key. I laughed a bit when the young woman took a deep breath and stood up a little straighter when I told her the name. I assured her it was a fake name and that I was in no way related to the famed hotel magnate.

The rental car arrived right on time and as quickly as I could manage I went to the agency to fill out the necessary paperwork. I had errands to run, and I didn't want to feel pressed for time once I returned to the hotel. I needed to get several things, but I wanted to take my sweet time actually getting ready for the night.

My first stop was at a lingerie store. I found the skimpiest, trashiest getup and matching stiletto shoes. I also bought a skin-tight dress that barely covered anything. I wasn't sure I would be comfortable actually wearing it anywhere, but I had a plan to remedy that.

Next, I stopped at a drug store and purchased all the makeup I would need to make myself look completely different. I actually hate wearing makeup. It makes my face feel dirty. I don't think about my looks often. My mother hadn't worn much makeup, and I suppose I was lucky that I never felt any pressure to wear it myself. I was comfortable with the way I looked. It was not something that felt important to me anyway.

My last stop before returning to the hotel was at the liquor store. I bought a cheap bottle of vodka and a good bottle of bourbon. I was planning on drinking the vodka while I was getting ready for Chris. I wanted to be good and drunk by the time he got to the room. I don't like to get drunk, but when I was doing something as out of character for myself as I had planned for tonight, it was a necessary evil. I wasn't sure if the bourbon would be touched, but I could always drink it later. Once I was back at the hotel I turned on some music and dumped out the bag of makeup on the bathroom counter. I poured myself a drink and got to work. I had to watch some tutorials on YouTube to get the look I was going for. Applying makeup was not one of my stronger skill sets.

By the time I had finished applying what felt like a mask to my face, I had already finished off about half the bottle of vodka. I looked at the clock and realized that Chris should be arriving any minute. I grabbed the skanky getup from the bag laying on the bed and took it into the bathroom. I wasn't quite sure where all the straps were supposed to go, and I was laughing at myself while I was trying to get into it.

I was admiring myself in the mirror when I heard a light knock at the door. It opened before I had a chance to move. "Charity?" Chris closed the door at the same moment I was closing the door to the bathroom.

"I'll be out in just a minute," I yelled through the closed door. I grabbed the blonde wig and quickly pulled it into place. I didn't look at all like myself, and I was proud that I had been able to pull off the transformation in my drunken state. I put on the heels and downed one last shot to steady my nerves before stepping out of the bathroom. "Hey, you!" I didn't recognize the voice that came from my lips. I also stumbled a bit in the ridiculously high heels. Perhaps that last shot hadn't been the smartest idea.

Chris turned around and the look on his face was exactly what I had hoped it would be. It was a mixture of shock, confusion, and desire. "Is..." he stammered, "Is that really you?"

"Who else would I be?" I slowly made my way toward him. I don't think it came across as sexy as I had intended. It probably looked more like I was walking slowly to keep from falling over. I was regretting both the vodka and the shoes.

He was biting his lower lip, and I saw beads of sweat begin to form on his forehead despite the fact that it wasn't remotely warm in the room. My nipples were proof of that fact. "You might be a goddess. Are you a goddess?"

I lightly ran my fingers up his arm then wrapped my arms around him, pulling him against me. I leaned into him and whispered in his ear. "I might be a goddess. Is that what you want me to be?" I kissed his neck. "I can be whatever or whoever you want me to be. Just say the words."

He groaned. "What I need is for you to shut the fuck up." He grabbed my ass and lifted me up. I wrapped my legs around his waist. He walked to the foot of the bed and threw me down. I propped myself up and watched as he practically ripped his clothes off.

"Don't destroy your clothes." I laughed like a hyena. There wasn't anything resembling sexy about the laugh. "I was hoping to go to dinner later."

I'm not sure how to describe the sound that came from him. It was either a growl, grunt, or groan. Whatever the right word was, it was the sexiest sound I had ever heard come out of a man. He was making my attempts at appearing sexy seem completely inadequate. "You are dinner." He said it like it was an order, and I had every intention of complying.

NINE

By the time we came up for air, I was no longer feeling drunk. I wasn't capable of walking, but it didn't have anything to do with the amount of liquor I had consumed. For a long time, we laid in the bed without talking. I didn't think either of us had any idea what to say at that point. It wasn't awkward though. The silence was almost perfect.

When he finally got up to go to the bathroom I noticed there were deep scratches on his arms and back. I looked down at the bed and noticed that there was blood on the sheets. Housekeeping wasn't going to be happy with us. I would have to make sure to leave a hefty tip in the morning.

I looked at the clock and was stunned to see that it was after midnight. "Dammit!" I didn't mean to say it out loud, but I was so disappointed that I couldn't help myself.

Chris stepped back into the room. He was wiping his arms with a wet washcloth that was streaked pink. "What's wrong?"

"I was really hoping for a decent dinner tonight. I don't

think we're going to find anywhere worth a damn open at this hour." I looked down at the sheets again and got up to walk to where he was standing. I gently touched his arm, and I felt bad for what I had done to him. "Are you okay?"

He laughed and kissed my forehead. It was more intimate than I would have liked. "I'll be fine. The battle scars are totally worth it."

We were both still completely naked. I looked around to see where my wig had ended up. I didn't immediately see it. "Get dressed, then. I need food." I walked over and picked up his clothes off the floor.

"Yes, ma'am!" He followed me and took the clothes from my hands. "Where do you think we're going this late?"

I headed over to the closet where I had hung up the dress that I had bought for tonight. "We can go to the Waffle House for all I care. I just know that I need food in my stomach. I'm famished."

He had been getting dressed and hadn't noticed that I had squeezed myself into the ridiculously tight dress. When he turned around his mouth fell open. "Do you actually plan to go out in that?" He was genuinely shocked, and I found it hilarious.

"Why? What's wrong with it?" I probably had the biggest grin of my life on my face. I turned around to give him the full effect. I think half of my ass was hanging out of the dress.

He looked around the room and saw my jeans laying in the chair by the window. "Why don't you wear these?" He practically ran over to pick them up.

"Nope. I want to wear this." I walked over to him and

planted a kiss on him that almost made me forget about going to get something to eat. Almost. "Now, are you coming with me or am I going to be dining alone?" I sat down on the end of the bed and started putting the ridiculously high heels on.

He kneeled down in front of me and took over the task of strapping on the shoes. "If you plan on wearing these, I have no choice but to join you." He ran his hand up my leg and I felt chills run up my spine. What was this man doing to me? "I don't think you would make it down the hall to the elevator if I don't go with you to keep you from falling over."

"Are you sure you won't be embarrassed to be seen with me?" He was still kneeling in front of me. I took the opportunity to do my best Sharon Stone impression and parted my legs ever so slightly so that he would realize that I wasn't wearing any panties under the dress. "I know that I don't look like a proper southern lady."

He jumped up and started to pull my dress up. I swatted his hands away. "That's not fair!" He was whining, and it was beyond amusing.

"Oh well. No one said life was fair. If anyone told you that it was, they were lying to you, and it's kinda sad that you believed them." I adjusted my dress so that nothing was showing that would get me arrested when I walked outside. "I'm leaving now. I hope you're coming with me."

I grabbed my room key and shoved it into his pants pocket. He followed me out the door, and we made it to the elevator without me falling on my face. I guess it had been the vodka that had made me so unsteady in the shoes earlier. They actually weren't at all hard to walk in now that I wasn't drunk.

Once we were in the elevator, Chris tried to get handsy again. His hands were on my waist, then my ass. I smacked the back of one of his hands. His inability to hide how much he wanted me was sending me on a power trip. "Chris, if you don't stop I'm going to send you back to the room. You will not misbehave while we are out in public."

"Yes, ma'am." He sounded like a scolded child.

I turned toward him and had to make a concentrated effort to keep a straight face. "Don't do that. Don't sulk. You are not a child. I am not your mother. Don't call me ma'am."

He took a deep breath and stood up a little straighter. I could tell he was struggling with what to say next. "What do I call you then?"

"You can call me Rati." I was fairly certain that he would have no idea where the name came from. I was right.

"Rati? What the hell kind of name is that?" He was completely confused.

I was thankful that I had taken a mythology course while I was in college. "Rati is the Hindu goddess of lust and passion. She is known for her beauty and sensuality."

"It definitely fits. You should think about changing your name to that in real life." The elevator doors opened to the lobby as he said this. "Come Rati. Let me introduce you to waffles fit for a goddess." He grabbed my hand and led me out of the elevator.

Chris insisted on driving the half block to the Waffle House. I think he was terrified that I would end up face down on the pavement if we had walked. When we pulled into the parking lot, I waited for him to come around and open the car door for me. He acted as a shield while I straightened my dress so as not to be obscene.

We walked in and it felt as if every person in the restaurant turned to look at us. I suddenly became overly aware of how short my dress was and began pulling it as far down as I could without my boobs popping out of the top. I leaned in to whisper in his ear. "Is it just me, or are they all staring at us?"

"They aren't staring at us, they're staring at you." He didn't even try to be quiet with his answer. We sat in the first empty booth and he leaned over. Whispering now, he said, "What did you expect? I'm not saying it's right for them to judge, but you don't exactly look like anyone else in here. You stand out like a sore thumb."

I looked around the dining room and realized that he was absolutely right. There were only a couple of other women in the restaurant, but they definitely weren't dressed like me. Every one of them was wearing jeans. I sat up straight, mostly to negate the feeling of immense self-consciousness that was threatening to overcome me.

"Well, if you've got it, flaunt it." I made sure that I spoke loudly enough for everyone to hear me. I looked around, and everyone in the place had suddenly begun whispering to the person sitting closest to them. "Not everyone is a goddess."

Chris laughed and leaned across the table. He wrapped his hands in my hair and pulled me into another intense kiss. I wasn't sure that we were going to make it to the ordering part of this meal. "Dammit, woman." He quickly corrected himself. "Dammit, Rati! You may be the most amazing being I have ever met."

"Settle down. We need to eat. I'm going to be pissed if we

get kicked out of here. You don't want me to take out my wrath on you when I'm hungry." I was really talking to both of us. I was having a hard time concentrating because I knew exactly how badly he wanted me. I wanted him just as much.

The waitress finally made her way over to the table. She looked irritated. "I'm sorry, ma'am," Chris said in the sweetest voice he could muster. "I promise we won't be any trouble. We won't make a scene. We just need to get some food in our stomachs."

She laughed, and her whole body shook. She was easily in her sixties, and I imagined that she had probably been working here for longer than I had been alive. "Don't worry about it, sugar. The customers may be a bunch of nosey busy-bodies, but I don't give a shit what you do as long as I don't have to see any stray body parts flailing around."

I decided it was best to let him handle this particular interaction. I didn't speak sassy southern grandma. I was out of my element.

"There definitely won't be any of that." He looked at me. "Are you ready to order, Rati?"

She gasped. "What the hell kinda name is Rati? Are you callin' her a rat?" She was genuinely offended for me. This woman had spunk and I liked it.

"Absolutely not! It's an inside joke, and I assure you it's a term of endearment. I wouldn't dream of insulting her." He was scared she was going to yell at him. I could see it in his eyes.

She looked at me for confirmation. "It's what I prefer that he call me. I like it." I smiled at him and looked back at her. "I would like two scrambled eggs with cheese and a double order of hash browns."

"Anything in those?" She didn't seem completely convinced that I was being honest with her, but she had switched into work mode, so she let it go.

I had to look at the menu to make sure that I used the correct terms to order my hash browns the way I liked them. I hadn't eaten at a Waffle House in years. "Yes, please. I'd like them chunked, covered, and country. I'd also just like water to drink, please."

"I'll have exactly the same as her." Chris looked at the waitress sheepishly. She shook her head at him and walked away.

We spent the next two hours in that Waffle House laughing and talking. I hadn't had that much fun in a very long time. I didn't want to admit to myself that I really liked Chris. He was funny and smart. Nothing about him seemed fake. I didn't want to like him. It didn't fit in with my plan.

When we got back to the hotel Chris decided to take a shower. I stripped off the dress and crawled onto the bed. I hadn't planned to fall asleep, but that's exactly what happened. I didn't wake up until my alarm went off at seven o'clock.

TEN

I woke up with Chris wrapped around me. It felt nice. It felt wrong. This wasn't what I needed. This wasn't what I wanted. I managed to get out of the bed without waking him. I stumbled into the bathroom still groggy. I needed more sleep.

I hopped in the shower, hoping that the ridiculously hot water would help me to shake off the drowsiness and slight hangover. This was definitely not the day for me to not be on top of my game. I stood under the shower head without moving at first. It felt amazing. I looked down and laughed as I noticed the blend of colors in the water at my feet. I had somehow managed to forget how much makeup I had put on last night.

By the time I stepped out of the shower I felt properly refreshed. The desire to go back to bed had been completely erased. In its place, the absolute resolve to get Chris out of this room so that I could begin to prepare for what would be the biggest day of my life to date. I wasn't sure how I was going to manage to get him to leave.

I wrapped myself in one of the plush towels and walked out of the bathroom. I looked around but didn't see Chris anywhere. Could I possibly be this lucky? Had he actually left of his own volition? Was I off the hook for trying to figure out how to get him to leave?

I grabbed the clothes I had been wearing yesterday and got dressed. I couldn't believe that I hadn't remembered to bring a fresh set of clothes for today. I decided that I liked this room too much and that I wouldn't be spending another night at the bed bug hotel. I called down to the front desk and was beyond pleased when they said that this room was available for the next two nights. I went ahead and booked it so that I wouldn't have to concern myself with checking out today. I had more important things on my plate for the day.

I picked up the shreds of the lingerie that were strewn around the room and tossed them in the garbage can. I decided that I was going to keep the dress and shoes. I felt powerful and sexy in them. I was Rati in them. I enjoyed being Rati. I had to shake off the memories of last night. I didn't have time to dwell on it. It was over. I had managed to have some fun, but now it was time to get down to business.

I made sure that the room was presentable for housekeeping and left a ten dollar bill along with a note apologizing for the sheets on the bed. I grabbed my wallet, room key, and keys to the rental car as I headed toward the door. I needed to go to the other hotel to get my things. I had a few errands I needed to run today as well. I was changing up the plan a bit, but I tried not to dwell on the thought that last minute changes were probably a bad idea.

I opened the door to find Chris on the other side picking

his room key up off the hallway floor. He looked up at me and smiled. "Good morning! I got us some breakfast." He held up a greasy brown paper bag. "Are you hungry?"

"I was actually just leaving." Dammit! I thought I had gotten out of this! I had to admit that whatever was in that bag smelled delicious though. I pushed the door back to let him in the room. "I guess I've got time to eat. We'll have to make it quick."

He set the bag down on the table and began pulling several items out of it and laying them out for me like a buffet. "I wasn't sure what your preference was for breakfast food, so I brought you a selection to choose from." He waved his arm over the table like one of the women on The Price is Right. "Pick your poison."

"Any chance there is a plain sausage biscuit in there somewhere? I'm fairly simple when it comes to food in the morning. Anything too heavy, and I won't feel like doing anything for hours." I walked over to the table to see what offerings he had brought for his goddess. I was going to have a hard time letting go of that detail from last night. I found the desired sausage biscuit and began devouring it.

Chris literally belly laughed. "Damn, woman. You have no shame when it comes to eating, do you?"

"Nope," I mumbled with a mouth full of biscuit. Chris had also brought a couple of cold bottles of water back with him. I grabbed one of them and chugged about half the bottle before trying to talk again. "What would be the point? I am who I am. Take me or leave me. It won't hurt my feelings in the least."

Chris licked his lips. "I'll take you right now if you'll let me." He was dead serious.

The way he said it made me want to strip off my clothes and throw myself at him. He was hard to deny, but I didn't have the time for playing today. "Sorry. I can't. I've got a million things to do today, and if I don't get started soon, I won't get them done."

"Well, that just plain sucks." He was giving me actual puppy dog eyes. He could have been in a commercial for the ASPCA he looked so pitiful. "How about tonight, then? I could take you to a proper dinner and everything."

"Sorry, but I already have dinner plans for tonight." I shoved the last bite of biscuit in my mouth and finished off the bottle of water. I decided now was the time to put an end to this. "Truthfully. This is going to be the last you see of me. Today is going to be a very long day, and I have an early flight home in the morning." The part about the flight was a lie, but the rest of what I had said was true.

You would have thought I had jammed a dagger directly into his heart. "Really? The last memory of you I'm going to have is of you shoveling a sausage biscuit down your throat?"

"Yeah. That's just the way it worked out. It's your fault, though. You brought the biscuits." I couldn't believe the words that had come out of my mouth. Why was I joking with him? There was no reason for me to be nice to him at this point. I needed him gone. Acting like this was going to give him hope. There was no hope.

He slowly pushed himself up off the bed. He was fidgeting. This wasn't a good sign. "Well, if you change your mind, you have my number." He headed directly to the door but stopped before leaving. "I really hope you change your mind."

I didn't turn around to watch him leave. I didn't want to see him go. I heard the door close, and that's when it hit me. He was gone. This was what I had wanted. This was what I had needed. No matter how true those things were, though, they didn't stop me from feeling as if I had just made one of the biggest mistakes of my life. There was a part of me that already missed him.

I didn't have time to dwell on it, which was definitely a good thing. I put the remaining biscuits in the trash can. I knew that I wouldn't eat them later. I realized that he hadn't even managed to eat one. I shook the thought of him off, grabbed my things, and headed out the door. I needed to get busy.

The first thing I did was drive back to the River Run Inn. I gathered all of my things and put them in the rental car. I had to make sure to double check that I hadn't left anything important in the room before I checked out. I was glad that I had made it a habit to always do that because the prescription bottle I had brought with me had fallen out of my bag and was under the edge of the dresser. I would have had to change the plan again if I had left it. There would have also been the not-so-small detail of my name on a medicine bottle in a room that wasn't registered under my real name. It could have easily come back to haunt me.

Next on the agenda was a visit to a local charity. This was something that I had been wanting to do for a long time. It had nothing to do with the Poppock plan. I wanted to make a donation because I loved the work that they do there. They are called the Magic City Sisters of Perpetual Indulgence. The name alone was enough to make me an instant fan. They work a lot with the LGBTQIA community with a strong focus on AIDS outreach.

I found their office and talked to several of the sisters about their work. I had a great time, and their passion for their work was evident in everything they said and did. I think I floored them when I pulled a cashier's check out for one hundred thousand dollars and handed it to them. I wanted to make sure that they had the funding they needed for the wonderful work they were doing. There were lots of hugs and a few tears shed before I left. It was a good feeling, but it wasn't one that would last.

I knew that I needed a few more things for tonight, but I needed to hit multiple stores to get them so as not to look suspicious. I had brought most of what I needed with me, but the change in the plan required more. I decided it would be safer to drive out of the immediate area to get them. It was almost noon, so I had about five hours before I needed to actually start getting everything together for tonight. I went back to the Hilton and took all of my things up to my room.

Once I had everything put away, I left again and found my way to the interstate. I drove for about an hour before I started looking for an exit that suited my needs. Finding one with a hardware store within sight, I pulled off the interstate. I went into the store and picked up the strongest roll of duct tape I could find.

I got back in the car and did a quick Google search for a nearby beauty supply store. There was one three exits up from where I was at, so I headed in that direction. I decided to stop at the next exit first, though because I was hungry by this point and I also needed to put some gas in the car.

I found a small bar-b-que joint along the main strip. From the outside, it didn't look like anything special, but I knew that the south was famous for their hole-in-the-wall restaurants. There was smoke billowing out from behind the building, and it smelled amazing. My mouth started watering before I even walked in the door.

The inside was like nothing I had ever seen. The walls were covered with framed newspaper articles featuring the restaurant. I walked around and looked at every one I could get to. It was like being in a museum. Some of the articles were over thirty years old. One of them was as recent as last month. This place was a goldmine of nostalgia.

I placed my order at the counter and looked around for a seat. There weren't many to choose from. The place was packed. My guess was that most of these people knew each other by name and that the employees knew their orders by heart. Every minute I spent inside warmed my cold, dead heart.

After some of the best food I had ever eaten, I stopped to get gas. While I was in the convenience store I also bought a lighter. It was a butane lighter that looked like a torch. I hadn't planned on getting one, but when I saw it I realized that it could come in handy tonight. I smiled at the thought of what I might use it for. Then I wondered if there was a part of me that was actually evil.

I made my way to the beauty supply store next. I wasn't getting a wig this time, but I did look at them and made a mental wish list of what style I wanted to get next. I found my way to the supplies used for dying hair. There I found exactly what I was looking for: heavy duty gloves. They were a must-have for tonight, and I wasn't sure how I had managed to overlook getting them earlier.

I had everything I needed now so I headed back toward Birmingham. As I drove, I sang along to the music on the radio and took in the beauty that surrounded me. The trees on the mountains were several different shades of deep green. They flowed together to make the trees appear as if they had green waves in them. It looked like something out of a painting. There was nothing like this back home.

I returned to the hotel just before four o'clock. I immediately got to work getting everything in order for my meeting with Daniel Poppock. Most of the work entailed going over the plan in my head and double checking to make sure that I had everything that I needed to pull it off. I took the anxiety meds and crushed all of them up into a fine powder. I put the powder in a small container that would fit in my pocket. Everything else went into the oversized purse that I had purchased solely for this undertaking.

Everything was now organized, and I found myself exhausted. The combination of not enough sleep last night and the multiple errands I had run today had crept up on me. I laid out my clothes for this evening, stripped off what I was currently wearing, and crawled under the covers for a nap. I set an alarm on my phone to wake me up at six o'clock. That would give me time to take a shower and pull myself together before leaving the hotel.

It couldn't have taken more than a couple of minutes for me to fall asleep. The sleep wasn't peaceful. I dreamt of death.

The first death was Daniel Poppock's. I was the one killing him, but it wasn't the way I planned to do it. We were fighting, and I was stabbing him with a huge knife. It was bloody and messy, and difficult. None of those things were part of the plan. When I left his house, I knew that I had left DNA and fingerprints and that I would be caught. The dream then jumped to me returning home. I was still covered in his blood, but for some reason, it didn't bother me at all. I walked into my house and called for Gayle and the dogs. There was no answer.

I noticed that there was a piece of paper on the coffee table in the living room. It didn't belong there. There was never anything on that table. I crept over and picked it up to read it.

I knew you were coming for me. I let you do it, but I killed you first.

- D.P.

It didn't make any sense. How would he have known? What did he mean when he said he killed me first? I couldn't figure it out, and I was beginning to panic. I dropped the note and began running through the house. I was frantically trying to find Gayle and the dogs. She should have been home by now. Where was she?

I was running from room to room looking for Gayle. I was oblivious to the fact that I was leaving bloody handprints on the doors and walls as I searched. She wasn't in any of the bedrooms, and she wasn't in the basement. I ran back toward the kitchen. She wasn't there, but the back door was open. Had she simply gone outside with the dogs and forgotten to close the door behind her? I instinctively knew that wasn't the case.

I noticed the smell as soon as I stepped outside. The gruesome scene in front of me was more than I could handle. I threw up almost immediately. Their bodies were in the fire pit. There wasn't much left of them, but there was no doubt it was them. The fire was still smoldering. I fell to the ground. This was it. He had done exactly what the note had said. He hadn't taken my life, but by killing Gayle and the dogs he had effectively killed me.

None of it made any sense. I simply couldn't comprehend how he had managed to pull it off. I was on the ground sobbing. I didn't know what to do. I was going through the options in my head when I heard the voice from behind me yell, "Put your hands up! Don't you fucking move!" I turned my head and saw Logan standing there with a gun pointed at me. I knew it was all over.

I woke up with a jolt. I was crying. That dream was the last thing I needed right now. It had completely rattled me. I looked at the clock and realized it was five minutes until six. I went ahead and turned off the alarm I had set earlier. The nap had ultimately been a horrible idea. I was exhausted and stressed now.

I took a shower, though it did little to lessen the tension in my body. I considered taking a shot of the bourbon that was still unopened on the table but decided that was a bad idea as well. I walked over and picked up the clothes I had picked out for tonight. Getting dressed was the only thing I knew to do at this point.

I went back into the bathroom and put on some makeup.

It wasn't the glam-job I had done last night. Tonight's look was simple and innocent. I needed to come across as exactly that. I had to be able to take him by surprise.

While I was applying my makeup, I heard a notification from the throw-away cell phone. It took me a second to even realize what the sound was. I pulled the phone from the purse and just stared at the screen. It was a message from Chris. I chose not to open it. It was one more thing that I simply couldn't deal with in this moment. I turned the phone off and shoved it back into the purse before returning to the bathroom to finish my makeup.

I got dressed and scrutinized myself in the mirror. I looked good in the jeans and cardigan. It wasn't something I would normally wear, but it suited me nonetheless. I grabbed the short brown wig and put it on as well, completing the look. I definitely didn't look like I normally do. Even Gayle wouldn't realize it was me right away.

Gayle. I missed her. I needed to do this right tonight. I needed to get back home to her. I wasn't going after Poppock *for* her, but I was going to make damn sure I did it *right* for her. If I got caught it would devastate her. She would feel as if she had failed me somehow. I was like one of her own children, and she would feel like she had failed as a parent the same as if I was her biological child.

I looked at the clock. It was time for me to leave. I grabbed the purse and left the room. When I got on the elevator there were several other people already on it. It was the most crowded I had seen it thus far. I felt like everyone was looking at me. Realistically, I knew that they weren't, but that was exactly how it felt. I was struggling to keep my composure. I actually breathed an audible sigh of relief when the elevator came to a stop and the doors opened to the lobby. I hoped that if anyone had been paying attention that they assumed I was claustrophobic instead of suspicious.

I got to the rental car and gave myself a pep talk before starting the engine. "You can do this. You have to do this. This is the right thing to do. Don't chicken out now. You've been preparing for this for months. You are ready."

The pep talk worked. I had calmed down significantly by the time I pulled out of the parking lot. I made my way to the shopping center where I planned to park the car. I stopped at the gas station on the corner first, though. I bought a six-pack of Heineken that I had absolutely no intention of actually drinking.

I parked the car at the shopping center and checked the purse one last time to make sure I hadn't forgotten anything. There was enough room left for me to put the beer in the purse as well. I took a deep breath before getting out of the car. I locked the car as I walked away. This was it. Now was the time. I wasn't turning back now.

ELEVEN

I found myself standing in front of Poppock's house at ten minutes till eight. I could smell the charcoal burning in the backyard. I took a deep breath to steady myself before walking around to the side of the house. I could hear music playing, though I wasn't sure exactly what genre it belonged to. He was standing at the grill dancing. It was an amusing sight for me. This man thought he was in for a good night. He thought he was going to get laid tonight. He thought he was going to brag to his buddies tomorrow about the hot chick he nailed. He had no idea just how wrong he was. He had no idea that the meal he was cooking was going to be his last.

I pulled the beer out of the purse and dangled it over the fence. "Hey, Danny!" I smiled the biggest smile I could manage as he turned around to see me. "You got somewhere I can put this before it gets hot?"

He hooked the long-handled tongs on the side of the grill and closed the lid. He danced his way over to the fence and let me in. It was one of the most ridiculous things I had seen in my life. If he was going to act like this all night, I wasn't going to have a problem taking him out. I was going to want to do it. "What kinda broke ass punk do you think I am that I ain't got no fridge to put your beer in?" He took the beer from me and started dancing back toward the house, only now the dancing movements were combined with the shake of a man that was clearly laughing.

Yup. This was going to be easy. I was settled down now. I knew I could handle this. I decided that I was going to take my time and try to enjoy it. I didn't even care that the thought made me feel evil.

"What's on the grill?" I yelled as I tried to catch up with him.

He was opening the sliding glass door that led from the concrete patio to the kitchen. "Nothin' special. Just my secret recipe chicken legs and some hot dogs." He motioned for me to follow him inside. I wondered what had made him decide on this particular meal. It didn't seem like the kind of thing someone cooks to impress someone else.

I stepped into the kitchen and was shocked by what I saw. "Wow! This is a great kitchen!" It was true. The thought ran through my mind that I should remodel my kitchen to look more like this.

"Why you sound so surprised, sweetheart?" He put the beer in the refrigerator and I was desperately hoping that he couldn't tell that calling me sweetheart made me cringe. "I got a nice house. Everything I do and have is nice."

I was fighting the urge to shut him down. The only thing that was keeping me from doing it was the knowledge that he would never torture another woman with this bullshit again. "I didn't mean it like that. I just really like how it's set up. It looks great." I walked over and inspected the countertops. "Are these marble?"

"Yes, ma'am. I wouldn't have anything less." He was looking me up and down like I was a piece of meat he might throw on the grill next to the chicken legs and hot dogs.

I wanted to keep looking at all the details in the kitchen, but I needed to see the rest of the house. I had to remind myself that I wasn't here to get tips for remodeling my own house. "I'm going to need to see the rest of this house. Would you mind giving me the tour?"

"Let me check on the food real quick, and I'll show you anything you want to see." The smile he flashed at me was creepy. There was no other word to describe it. He wasn't going to stop with this crap which was going to make keeping myself in check difficult. I've never been good at biting my tongue when something irritates me. "You stay right here. Don't try sneaking a peek. The tour isn't the same without the tour guide." He shimmied his way back out the door.

He was back in the kitchen faster than I had expected or wanted. I was beginning to struggle with the idea that I was going to have to spend at least the next couple of hours with this man. "That was quick." It was the only thing I could think to say.

"I didn't have to do anything. The meat is exactly where it's supposed to be right now." He hooked his thumbs into his belt, and his fingers were angled toward his groin. It was a classic move that a lot of men do when they want you to look toward their penis. It's pathetic, really. "It'll be done in about fifteen minutes. C'mon. I'll show you around." He didn't wait for me at all. He was out of the kitchen before I had even started moving. I had to walk quickly to catch up to him.

The rest of the house was as beautiful as the kitchen. Everything about it was the exact opposite of what I had originally expected. He was exactly what I expected, though. When he showed me his bedroom, he actually used the phrase, "this is where the magic happens." If you were searching for a picture of the type of man women generally classify as a pig, he would be the poster boy.

We made our way back to the kitchen. He headed to the door to go back outside. "Grab me a beer while I check on this food." He was serious! I couldn't believe that he actually said that to me. I wasn't mad, though. It was exactly the opportunity that I needed.

I opened the refrigerator and grabbed one of his beers and one of mine. There was a bottle opener magnet stuck to the front of the fridge. I grabbed it and popped both of them open. I looked toward the door to make sure that he couldn't see what I was doing. He had his back to me. I had to move quickly, though. I didn't know how long I had.

I poured my beer down the drain and filled the bottle with water from the tap. Next, I pulled the bag from my pocket and shook some of the powder from the crushed up pills into his bottle. I could only hope that he wouldn't be able to taste it.

I headed out and joined him on the patio. He had turned the music off and stopped dancing. Finally, something to be thankful for. I handed him the beer he had requested. He turned the bottle up and drank more than half of it before setting the bottle down on the table next to the grill. I was paying close attention to his face. If he had tasted the medicine, he didn't show it at all.

"You ain't from here, are ya?" He started pulling the hot dogs off the grill and placing them on a cookie sheet that was covered in aluminum foil. "You sound like a damn yankee."

Now, I know that the dialect in the south is different from up north. I don't have a problem with it normally. When Chris had spoken I had found the southern accent charming. That wasn't the case with Poppock. He sounded uneducated. He sounded stupid. Coming from him it was simply the butchering of the English language and was like nails on a chalkboard for me.

"No. I'm not from here. I guess I am a damn yankee." I know the term is supposed to be an insult, but it only made me think of the band that had been somewhat popular in the early nineties. Suddenly I had images of Ted Nugent in my head, and he was the last person I wanted to be thinking about right now.

He was now removing what appeared to be completely burnt chicken legs off the grill. I wasn't sure how I was going to eat this stuff. "Where ya from, then?" He picked up his beer and finished it off with one more good chug. Again, I didn't notice anything about his face that would suggest he thought it tasted off.

"Pennsylvania. Pittsburgh specifically," I lied. I was a horrible liar. I doubted that he was paying enough attention to my face to be able to tell. His gaze mostly landed on my breasts or my ass. "Are you originally from Alabama? Your accent is definitely heavy enough for you to be."

He picked up the tray with the burnt food and turned to go inside. "Yeah. Born and raised in sweet home Alabama."

I followed him inside. I tried to look for signs that the medicine was starting to work its magic. It always hit me quickly when I took it. I assumed it would be even faster when crushed into a powder. I was disappointed that I couldn't tell a difference in his demeanor yet.

He sat the tray down on the kitchen counter and pulled a couple of cheap plastic plates out of the cabinet. "I gotta go take a piss. Why don't you get the coleslaw and baked beans out of the fridge while I'm gone? There's silverware in that drawer." He pointed to the drawer under the dish drainer before disappearing down the hall.

I couldn't believe how obnoxious he was. I looked in the fridge and found the containers of coleslaw and baked beans. He had bought them from a grocery store deli. He couldn't even be bothered to make these two simple items himself. I shook my head in amazement. I placed them on the counter next to the burnt chicken and hot dogs. This meal was going to be miserable.

I took the opportunity to prepare another beer for him. This time I added a bit more of the medicine. I needed this man to become unstable quickly for my own sanity. When he walked back in the kitchen I handed it to him, but I noticed his movements seemed a bit wobbly. I mentally celebrated this small victory.

He took a long drink of the beer. At the rate he was going, he was going to be knocked out in no time. "I'm going to set up a couple of trays in the living room so we can watch

TV while we eat. Go ahead and fix yourself a plate." He wobbled his way out of the kitchen again and I wondered if he was going to be able to make it back.

I grabbed a plate and looked around the room once more. There were no hot dog buns to be seen. This dinner date would go down in the tacky date hall of shame. I picked through the hot dogs and chicken legs looking for the least burnt pieces. I pulled a couple of spoons and forks out of the drawer and scooped small portions of the beans and coleslaw onto my plate. It was by far the most unappetizing plate of food that I had ever seen.

He hadn't made it back yet, so I made my way to the living room. I was hoping that I would find him passed out on the couch, but he wasn't. He had set up two TV trays in front of the couch for us to eat at. He was standing in front of the tv flipping through the channels. "What'chu wanna watch?"

"Oh, I don't care. Whatever you pick is fine with me." I put my plate on one of the trays and sat down on the couch. It was really comfortable. "I wasn't sure how much of what you would want, so I didn't make you a plate." I took a sip of my water disguised as beer.

He stopped channel surfing when he found a baseball game. "I guess we'll watch the game." His words were slurred. He turned to go back to the kitchen. I noticed that he was no longer taking complete steps. He was shuffling across the floor. It was the same type of thing that a mother would get frustrated about before yelling at her child to pick up their feet when they walked. I considered saying exactly that to him.

My confidence was growing. He wasn't going to stay

upright much longer. I realized it was possible he wouldn't make it back to the living room. I jumped up from the couch and joined him in the kitchen. He had piled his plate high with the atrocities he called food. He was standing in front of the counter just staring at the plate.

I walked up behind him and put my hand on his shoulder to let him know I was there. "Why don't you go ahead and sit down. I'll bring your plate to you. Do you need another beer?"

He turned around and almost lost his balance. He steadied himself by putting his hands on my shoulders. I had to fight the instinct to ram my knee into his balls. "Yeah. I'll take another one." I barely understood what he said. He finished the beer that was in his hand and dropped the bottle into the sink. "You're a sweet girl. I like you." He moved like a sloth as he made his way back to the living room.

I grabbed another beer from the fridge for Daniel. For a moment I considered not adding any more of the powder to it. I knew that he was on the edge of succumbing to the medicine's effects. I decided to add a small amount just to be safe. I picked up his plate and joined him in the living room.

He was sitting on the couch, but he was leaning against the back, and his eyes were barely open. "Here you go!" I made sure my voice was perky and a higher pitch than was normal to pull him out of his trance. I put the food and beer on the tray in front of him.

"Thanks, doll." I noticed he was drooling now. He sat up as straight as he could manage and looked at his plate with dead eyes.

This was it. He was not far from being exactly where I

needed him to be. "I'm going to run to the bathroom and wash my hands. I'll be right back." I tapped my hand on the tray in front of him. "Eat up. You look like you could use it."

I went to the bathroom and washed my hands. By the time I made it back to the living room Poppock had passed out. He had fallen back on the couch, and he had a chicken leg in one hand that was laying in his lap. I laughed at the scene. I made a point of making noise as I moved across the room. I slid the tray away from him and the legs squeaked across the hardwood floor. He didn't move.

I thanked the gods that I had managed to get out of eating any of the food and grabbed my purse from the kitchen table. Now I had to get to work. The first thing I grabbed was the zip ties. I looped two of them together and quickly slipped them over his wrists. There was no movement from him as I tightened them so that he wouldn't be able to get out of them.

I checked to make sure he was still breathing. It would have sucked if he wasn't. I didn't want him to get away with a peaceful death. I leaned in toward his face. I could feel his breath on my cheek and it gave me chills. I wasn't going to get that close to his face again.

I plopped down on the floor and removed his shoes. I took two more zip ties and pulled them tightly around his ankles. Next, I checked his pockets to make sure there was nothing in them that he might somehow be able to use against me. I only found his cell phone and wallet. I turned the phone off and laid them on the coffee table before reaching back into the purse.

I took out the gloves and pulled on a pair. I wasn't sure

how long he would be out, but I hoped that it would be long enough to complete the cleaning I needed to do. I went into the kitchen and found bleach under the sink. I grabbed the washcloth that was in the sink and doused it with the bleach. I spent the next ten minutes wiping down every surface I had touched with the bleach. I wasn't one hundred percent certain that it would eliminate all of my fingerprints, but I had been fairly careful about what I had touched up to this point.

I took all of the food and threw it in the garbage can outside. I hand washed the dishes, then just to be extra careful, I put them in the dishwasher and turned it on. I grabbed one of the chairs from the kitchen table and took it into the living room. I hoped that I wouldn't struggle too much to get him into it.

I sat it next to the couch so that I wouldn't have to move him very far. He was still unconscious. I took off the gloves that I was wearing and tossed them into my purse. I replaced them with a fresh pair and grabbed the duct tape and scissors from the bag. The duct tape still had the plastic on it, and because of the gloves, I had to cut it off with the scissors. I realized this was going to be a pain in the ass because of the gloves, but I couldn't risk my fingerprints on anything else.

Making sure the tape and scissors were within reach in case I needed them quickly, I braced myself for moving him to the chair. I knew that the easiest way to move him was going to be to pull him up from under his arms. This was going to require that I get close to his face again. Realizing this, I decided it was best to cover his mouth. I didn't want to startle him awake and have him bite me while I was trying to move him.

I pulled a piece of tape from the roll and winced when it made the tearing sound that is unique to duct tape being pulled from the roll. My eyes darted to his face to make sure he wasn't stirring. I had forgotten how loud that sound was. I cut the piece off and gently placed it over his mouth. I breathed a sigh of relief when he started breathing through his nose but didn't wake up.

Now I was ready to move him. I twisted my neck from side to side as if that would somehow make the task easier. I leaned in and hooked my elbows under his armpits. Still no movement from him. It took all of my strength to shift him from the couch to the chair, but I managed to do it. I put my hand on his chest to hold him against the back of the chair. I reached over and grabbed the duct tape with my free hand.

I wrapped the tape around his chest, waist, and legs. He wasn't getting out of this chair unless I decided he was, and that wasn't going to happen. I noticed at one point that his eyelids were fluttering, and I wondered what he was dreaming about. What kind of dreams would a man like this have?

His lack of movement gave me time to go through his house. I wanted to find his stash. I knew it was there. I simply had to locate it. I figured he wouldn't go for any of the conventional hiding places, but I knew I needed to check them anyway.

I started in the living room. I doubted that I would find anything. The room was sparsely decorated. It looked good that way, though. There weren't many hiding places, and the few I found were empty.

My next stop was his bedroom. I looked under the bed and the mattresses. I dug through the nightstands and the oversized dresser. When I opened the closet door my mouth dropped. This man owned more clothes than me. The drug trade must be booming in Bama. I looked through every single shoebox in the closet, and trust me, there were a lot. I didn't find a single thing that would incriminate him. I started to question whether he was actually a drug dealer.

I walked out of the bedroom into the hallway. I had two choices. I could check the spare bedroom or the bathroom. I remembered from the tour he had given me earlier that there wasn't much of anything in the spare bedroom. I doubted he would have anything hidden in there. I chose to go to the bathroom instead.

I looked through the linen closet and found nothing out of the ordinary. The tank on the toilet was also clear. I opened the cabinet under the sink. There wasn't much in it. A few random cleaning products and some extra toilet paper. I shifted things around, and that's when I noticed it. There was an actual trap door built into the bottom of the cabinet. I opened it up and found the jackpot.

He had everything in there. There was meth, crack, heroin, and pills. For some reason, I found it odd that there was no marijuana. It wasn't legal on any level in Alabama, so it would still be in high demand on the streets there. I also found two handguns as well.

I gathered all of it and took it to the living room. I put it on the coffee table so that he would be able to see that I had found it when he woke up. I didn't know how long that would be. I was tempted to try to wake him up but decided instead to wait it out. I wanted to see the panic in his eyes as he slowly came to and realized that he was fucked.

I grabbed the remote for the television then pulled the recliner into a position where I could see his face and the TV at the same time. I walked through the house and made sure that all of the windows and doors were locked. I turned off all the lights except for one lamp in the living room and checked to see that all of the curtains were closed. Finally, I plopped down into the chair and pulled the handle so that I could put my feet up. I deserved to relax for a little while. I flipped through the channels, and when I came across *Snapped* on Oxygen, I took the hint and settled in for the wait.

TWELVE

It was almost two hours later before Poppock began to stir. I turned the television off so we would have no distractions. I brought another chair in from the kitchen and sat it directly in front of him. I grabbed my purse and laid it on the floor next to the chair as I sat down. We were face to face. I was just waiting for him to realize what was happening.

I saw it in his eyes the instant the fear hit him. It was the best high I had ever experienced. I was born for this. His terror-filled me with a joy that I couldn't compare to anything else. I felt the excitement build in me as the hairs on my arms stood on end. I smiled at him. "Hi, Danny boy! Did you have a nice nap?"

He struggled against the restraints I had put him in. He was desperately looking around the room, trying to put it all together. His eyes made their way to the coffee table, and I saw the horror intensify on his face. He looked back at me, and his expression changed to anger. He tried to yell at me, but it was suffocated by the duct tape.

"Oh, don't be angry. You brought this on yourself." My tone was sugary sweet and condescending. I leaned in close and whispered in his ear. "This is the day you pay for your transgressions." I stood up and grabbed him by the hair. Pulling his head back so that he was looking up at me, I made sure he knew that I was in charge and there was nothing he could do about it. "Now, are you going to take your punishment like a man, or are you going to cry like a baby?"

Again, he tried to yell at me. I laughed at his futile attempt and slapped him hard across the face. A red handprint appeared on his cheek instantly. I pulled the lighter and a knife out of the purse and showed him both. I had no intention of using the knife; cleaning up blood was not a part of my plan, but he would never know that. The lighter, on the other hand, was going to be used if he didn't cooperate.

I sat back down in front of him. "Please, don't do that thing where you think that just because I'm a woman I can't completely destroy you. I assure you, I can. Even if I hadn't already drugged you with enough Xanax to take down a horse, I could still take you out without much effort." I grabbed a corner of the tape covering his mouth. "I'm going to take this off now because I need you to be able to talk, but if you scream, even as I'm removing it, I'm going to slit your fucking throat. Do you understand?" He nodded his head.

I ripped the tape from his face in one quick motion. His face contorted as he tried not to scream, and his eyes filled with tears. "Why?" His voice was a whisper. "What did I ever do to you?" His words were still slightly slurred.

"This isn't about what you did to me. As far as I know,

you don't know anything about me or anyone I know. This is about what you've done to other people." There was something about my tone of voice that surprised me. I sounded truly evil. Perhaps I was. I wasn't going to think about that right now, though. I had more important things on my plate.

Tears were streaming down his face. For a man who had presented himself in such a confident manner, he was surprisingly pitiful. "Tell me what I did. Tell me how I can make it right. Please, just don't kill me. I'll do anything you ask." He was begging for his life.

"Oh. You want to negotiate? Okay, we can try that." I reached over and tapped my hand against his face softly. "Let's see if you can convince me that you deserve to live. I need you to tell me the truth about the murders you were charged with. Don't lie to me either. I already know what happened. I just need to hear you say it out loud."

He looked down at the floor. "Okay. Fine." He looked back up at me. I would have said anyone else looked guilty, but I didn't believe he was capable of feeling that emotion. "I did it. I did everything they said I did."

"So, you admit that you ordered the murder of five innocent people, including three children? That's what you're saying, right?" I started playing with the lighter, turning it on and off repeatedly.

There was rage in his eyes. "That fucker wasn't innocent! He took my stuff and never paid me for it! He fucking owed me!" There was fire in his eyes and venom in his voice.

I punched him hard in the nose. "I told you not to yell. That's the only warning you get."

Blood was running down over his lips. "You bitch!" He hissed at me. "You better hope I don't ever get my hands on you."

"Oh, sweetie. That's cute. Do you really think this night is going to end with you still being alive? I knew you were dumb, but that's on a whole new level." I stood up and walked behind his chair. I took the lighter and lit it next to his ear so he could hear it. "Now, this is going to hurt, but you aren't going to make a sound. This is your penance. This is how you pay for what you did to those kids." I placed the flame on his earlobe. He tensed up, and I could tell he was suppressing a scream.

I walked back around the chair and stood in front of him. "You handled that well. Only two more to go!" My voice accurately reflected the satisfaction I was getting from torturing him like this. I repeated the process of burning him on one of his fingers then on one of his elbows. By the time I stopped, he looked like he was going to puke. "Don't you go getting sick on me now. I can handle the smell of your burnt flesh, but vomit is going to be a bit much for me."

"Please stop! I'm begging you!" He was sobbing, and his words were broken. "Take me to the cops. I'll tell them everything. I'll do my time! Just please make this stop!"

I ruffled his hair and pinched his cheek. "Aww. Does the wittle boy want the pain to stop? Do you need me to call your mommy? I will, you know. She should hear about how you didn't hesitate to kill those people." I plopped back down in the chair and tossed the lighter and knife back in the bag.

"Why are you doing this to me? I told you what you wanted to hear." He was trying to hide the fact that he was still crying, but his shoulders were shaking, and it gave him away.

I wrapped one hand around his throat and squeezed. "This isn't about you. This is about justice for those people and their families. The problem right now is that I don't think your confession is complete." I shoved him a little as I removed my hand from his neck. The chair wobbled beneath him. "We've established that you had that family killed. It's also quite obvious that you sell practically every deadly illegal drug there is. That's not all of it, is it?"

"No." He dropped his head. "I killed Monty too." He started sobbing. These were genuine tears, and I was taken aback.

"Wait. Monty? That was the guy you paid to kill them, right?" I leaned back in the chair and studied him for a moment. "I had been pretty sure that you were responsible for his death too, but I don't get why you feel bad about it. What did he mean to you?"

He lifted his head and looked at me as if I had just kicked a puppy. "He was my brother. Not my real brother, but we had been friends since we were too little to remember." His chest was heaving as he choked out the words. "I didn't mean to kill him. I gave him the wrong stuff. The heroin I gave him was laced with fentanyl. He was supposed to get the regular stuff. It was my fault he died. I loved him."

"Interesting. Somehow, I believe you." I crossed my arms over my chest. "I really hate that for you. It must suck knowing that you are directly responsible for the death of your best friend."

He completely broke down when I said that. He was

trying to say something, but it was completely incomprehensible. He took a few deep breaths and composed himself. "That's everything, I swear. Can we end this now? Just call the cops already."

"How many times do I have to tell you that you aren't going to live through this night? Did you think I would change my mind once you gave me the sob story about Monty? That doesn't change anything. You are going to die tonight. No amount of crying or begging is going to keep that from happening." I leaned in toward him so that our faces were only a couple of inches apart. I looked him squarely in his eyes. "Do you understand that now? Is it clear that I am going to kill you?"

He spit in my face. "You fucking bitch!"

I kicked his chair, and it fell over. His head hit the floor and started bleeding. I shook my head. "Now look at that. You forced me to make you bleed again. I really was hoping that I wouldn't have to do that again." I wiped the spit from my face and slammed my foot down on the side of his head.

I pulled the chair back into an upright position. I looked him over. He looked like absolute shit. If I hadn't known what kind of man he was, I might have felt sorry for him. Unfortunately for him, I knew exactly what kind of man he was, and he would get no pity from me. "Are we on the same page now? Do you comprehend what's actually happening here?" I sat back down in my chair.

"Yes. I get it." He sounded defeated. He knew that he was done. "Can we just get it over with?"

I reached down into the purse and pulled out a small brown paper bag. "We'll get to that in a minute. First, I have a surprise for you. Would you like to take a guess at what I have in this bag?"

"I don't know." He had resigned himself to his fate and no longer cared what was going to happen next. I was fairly certain he was going to change his mind about that momentarily.

I stuck my hand in the bag and removed the package inside. I was careful to make sure he couldn't see what it was. "I'm particularly proud of this. It doesn't matter how I got them, but I managed to get my hands on your medical records. There was some interesting information in there." His eyes grew larger and he gasped as the realization hit him. "That's right, Danny! You're deathly allergic to peanuts. Can you imagine how thrilled I was to find out that all I had to do to kill you was bring some peanut butter with me to your house?"

"Please! Please don't!" I found it amusing that the thought of not being able to breathe had suddenly brought back his will to live.

I unwrapped the package and showed him what was inside. A simple plastic spoon full of peanut butter. "Now, I'm going to do you one small favor. I'm going to cut the ties off of your hands. Don't bother trying to grab me when I do. It'll be pointless. I'm only allowing you to have your hands free for my own amusement."

With my finger, I smeared the peanut butter across his upper lip. Next, I grabbed the scissors and cut the zip ties that had held his hands together. He didn't try to grab me. I had known that he wouldn't. He immediately brought his hands to his face and started trying to wipe the peanut butter off. It didn't matter, and we both knew it.

The adrenaline flowing through him seemed to speed up the reaction. He quickly broke out into hives. It only took about a minute for me to notice a marked difference in his breathing. He began clawing at his face and neck. I simply stood back and watched until he started turning blue. This was the moment I had been waiting to experience for months.

"Danny. Danny!" He looked up at me. He was barely breathing. "I need you to understand that this is what you deserve. This is your karma coming back to bite you in the ass. It's a shame, really. If you had only chosen to be a decent human being, karma wouldn't have had to be such a bitch to you."

I stood and watched as his breathing slowed even further, and he lost consciousness. I waited until I couldn't see or hear any signs that he was still breathing before checking for a pulse. He had one, but only barely. I cut the tape off of him and moved him back to the couch. I laid him down and removed the zip ties from around his ankles. I crammed all of the restraints back into the purse. I looked around to make sure there was nothing else laying around that I had brought into the house. Once I was satisfied that I had my things cleaned up, I went back to check to see if he was still alive.

He wasn't. I laid my head against his chest to be sure. There were absolutely no signs that he was breathing or that his heart was beating. I had done it. I had killed him.

I was thankful that I had prepared myself for the emotions that came over me as I took in the scene before me. I had known that I would freak out, but I had also told myself that when I did I would have to simply push those emotions to the back of my mind and deal with them later. I didn't have time to have a breakdown right now. I had to finish up in the house and get the hell out.

I decided to do one more wipe down of the things I had touched before I put the gloves on. I knew that I had time. The house was dark, and from the outside, I was sure it looked like no one was home. I remembered that the beer I had brought was still in the fridge. I grabbed it and took it back into the living room. I checked one last time to make sure he was dead. Satisfied that he was, I slung the purse over my shoulder.

I noticed that his wallet and phone were still laying on the side table. I took them as well, remembering that I had pulled them from his pants before I had put the gloves on and knowing that they most likely had my fingerprints on them. I was fairly certain that was everything. It was time for me to leave.

I left out the same way I had come in. I quietly made my way out of the yard and walked nonchalantly down the street. In my head, I was terrified that someone was going to notice me walking through the neighborhood. I had to make myself walk at a slower pace than I wanted. Every ounce of me wanted to run. Considering what I was wearing, that would have definitely looked out of place if someone had seen me. It took me about twenty minutes to get back to the shopping center where my rental car was parked.

I opened the trunk of the car and placed the purse inside. I pulled out my wallet and my real cell phone in case I needed them. I got in the car and pulled out of the parking lot quickly. I needed to get out of the area. I knew that the chances were slim that Poppock would be found quickly, but there was always the chance that someone had seen me leaving his house and called the police about a suspicious person in the neighborhood.

THIRTEEN

I drove mindlessly around Birmingham for the next hour. I was completely lost by the time I pulled into a random Waffle House parking lot. I set the GPS to get me to the airport. I pulled into short-term parking and took the purse out of the trunk. I walked to where I had parked my car when I had arrived in town and placed the bag in the trunk. I decided I would deal with getting rid of everything on the trip back home.

Before I closed the trunk, I realized that Poppock's cell phone could be a problem, so I took it out of the purse. I walked back to the rental car, turning his phone over in my hand the entire way. I still had the gloves on my hands. I hadn't realized that I had failed to take them off until I was sitting in the car again, looking at his phone. I was trying to figure out exactly what to do with it. I opened up the back of the phone to remove the battery and the sim card. For the time being, that would be sufficient.

I left the airport and made my way back to the Hilton.

When I got out of the car I shoved his phone and its parts in my back pocket. I grabbed my phone and wallet and headed toward the front door. I finally removed the gloves and tossed them into the garbage can in the lobby. I made my way to the elevator and was relieved when the doors opened and it was empty.

Somewhere between the lobby and my room I turned into a zombie. I walked into the bathroom and stripped off my clothes. I climbed into the shower. I made sure the water was as hot as possible, and I scrubbed every inch of myself as if I had been doused in something toxic. By the time I stepped out, my skin was an unnatural shade of red. I didn't even bother grabbing a towel to dry off. I didn't want anything touching me.

I looked down at the pile of clothes on the floor at my feet. Poppock's phone was sticking out of the pocket of my jeans. For some reason, the sight of it filled me with rage. I snatched it from the pants and tossed it into the room next to the bed. I looked around the room trying to find something to smash it with. I saw the stilettoes in the closet and dashed across the room to get them. I dropped to my knees by the phone and slammed the spikey heel directly in the center of the phone's screen. It shattered, and I felt such a sense of satisfaction that I continued slamming the heel into the phone for what felt like an eternity.

When I finally stopped, I was out of breath and the phone was in hundreds of pieces scattered across the floor. I sat and stared at it. I was frozen and didn't know what to do next. I felt a weight fall over me, and I wasn't sure that I would be able to move if I tried. I honestly don't know how long I sat there like that, but I finally got the nerve to try to move and was surprised when I was able to stand.

I looked over at the clock on the nightstand. It was almost three o'clock. The entire night was a blur, and I couldn't pinpoint what I had done at any given time. I knew what I had done, but it didn't feel like it had taken seven hours to do it all.

I turned out all the lights and crawled under the covers. Normally, I would have turned on the television to help me sleep. I've always had a hard time sleeping in hotel rooms if the TV wasn't on. I didn't need it tonight. I was physically and mentally exhausted. I had nothing left. I passed out, and I didn't wake up until housekeeping knocked on my door.

I bolted out of the bed and wrapped myself in one of the sheets. I got to the door just as the housekeeper was beginning to open it. I apologized and let her know that I wouldn't be needing any service today. Once she was gone I dragged myself back over to the bed and sat down. I wasn't sure how to classify how I was feeling. I had expected to be filled with guilt or fear at this point. There was even a small part of me that thought I might feel relief or satisfaction. I didn't feel any of those things. The only thing I was feeling now was the need to go home.

I hadn't planned on leaving town this quickly, but it was what I decided I was going to do. I called the rental car company to see if it would be okay for me to return the car to the airport location. They confirmed that it would be fine, so I packed up my things. I scraped up as much of the phone carnage as I could manage and tossed it into the wastebasket. This was the end of this journey. I had completed my mission.

I made my way to the airport to return the rental car and retrieve my own. It didn't take long, and it was nice to be driving my vehicle again. I felt like myself for the first time in days, but I couldn't shake the feeling that I had forgotten something, and I couldn't figure out what it could possibly be.

I decided to take my time on the drive home. I wasn't in any hurry. Gayle wasn't going to be home for two more days, and she wasn't expecting me until two days after she returned. I had time to kill. I laughed at the thought. I needed to stop using that saying.

Once I made it to Nashville I got off the interstate. I wanted to actually see the towns I was driving through. The most interesting things are always found well off the interstate. Each stop I made along the way, whether it be for food, gas, or just something interesting I came across, I tossed a piece of evidence in a trash can.

For the next three days, I drove from town to town finding interesting things to see and do. I spent the majority of one day making several stops along the Kentucky Bourbon Trail. I had always wanted to visit. My love for bourbon made it the perfect tourist attraction for me.

I also stopped in Cincinnati and visited their zoo. I didn't like it as much as the one in Toledo, but it was nice. Afterward, I stopped at a Skyline Chili and had a couple of their famous hot dogs. They definitely lived up to the hype.

I made a point of staying off the Internet. I wasn't ready to find out what had come of my dirty deed. It was nice. I thoroughly enjoyed my trip.

Gayle texted me Monday morning to let me know that she was headed home, then later that day to let me know that she had made it safely and the house was fine. I told her that I would be home tomorrow instead of Wednesday. I was ready to see her.

By the time I pulled into my driveway I was completely relaxed. Gayle must have heard me pull in because, by the time I stepped out of the car, Lilith and Loki were bounding toward me. Gayle wasn't far behind them. She looked great. The time with her family had obviously done her a lot of good.

We spent the evening talking about what we had each done over the last week. Obviously, everything I told her was a lie. I absolutely hated myself for lying to her, but it was for her own protection. If she knew what I had done, it would destroy her.

After a long night of storytelling and laughs, we finally went to bed around midnight. It had been a long time since the two of us had spent time together like that. I made a mental note to make sure to make it happen more frequently. It was good for both of us. I crawled into my bed and slept better than I had in months. I felt no guilt and no anxiety. The deed was done, and there was nothing that anyone could do to change it. There was no reason to worry about if it would come back to haunt me. What was done was done. My mother used to say, "You can't put the toothpaste back in the tube." It was very true.

I woke up Wednesday morning feeling completely refreshed. Being home was the best feeling in the world. I went to my office and grabbed my laptop. I wanted to spend some time outside with Gayle and the dogs today. I was pleasantly surprised to find that she had thought of it already.

She was sitting outside at the patio table with a cup of coffee. Lilith and Loki were in the yard playing tug-o-war with a giant stick.

I made my way to the table and laid down the laptop. "Does your coffee need to be topped off? I'm about to make myself a cup."

"No dear. I'm good. It's a beautiful morning, isn't it?" She was looking off in the distance. I don't think she was looking at anything in particular, just taking in the view.

"It definitely is." I went back inside to make my cup of coffee and quickly rejoined her at the table. "I think I'm going to spend the day out here. It's too nice to be cooped up in the house."

Gayle nodded her head in agreement. "It's too nice to be running errands too, but unfortunately that's exactly what I need to do." She moved her chair away from the table and stood up.

"No! I was hoping we could spend the day together." I didn't want her to leave my sight. She was one of the best things about being home.

She patted me on the shoulder as she walked by. "I won't be gone long. I've got some dry cleaning to pick up, and we really need some groceries if we aren't planning on starving ourselves." Her voice softened a bit, and I struggled to hear as she said, "I'm also stopping by the police station to drop off a thank you gift for Logan. It was nice of him to keep an eye on the house while we were gone." She quickly stepped into the house. She had hoped that I hadn't actually heard what she had said.

"Wait a minute!" I jumped up and ran in after her. "You're

going to see Logan?"

She sighed and rolled her eyes at me. "Yes. I'm going to see Logan. A thank you gift is in order when someone does you a favor. I can't have him thinking I've forgotten my manners."

"What did you get him as a gift, if you don't mind me asking?" I was dying to know.

She blushed. The suspense was killing me. "It's just a gift card to the Italian restaurant downtown. I know he likes to eat there."

"Who do you think you're fooling? *You* like to eat there! You're hoping he'll ask you to join him for dinner!" I was stunned by her cunning plan. It was actually quite brilliant. "Don't lie. Tell me the truth. That's what you're hoping for, isn't it?"

Her face was beet red. She knew I was right. "Fine. Yes, that's what I'm hoping for. I decided while I was gone that I needed a little more life in my life. I'm boring, and I don't want to be any longer."

"I wouldn't say you are boring, but I'm glad you are at least trying to spice things up a bit." I grabbed her and squeezed her with every ounce of strength I had. "Now, you run along and get yourself that man in uniform. That's what you like about him, isn't it?"

She swatted me away and laughed. "That's not all I like about him, but it certainly doesn't hurt." She picked her purse up off the kitchen counter. "I'm leaving now. I'll fill you in when I get back. I shouldn't belong."

"Good luck!" I yelled as she closed the door behind her. I made my way back out to the patio table and sat down. I opened up my laptop. Four days of avoiding the Internet had been long enough. I needed to know what was happening in Birmingham. I took a deep breath before entering Poppock's name into the search bar.

I only found a couple of articles about his death. Apparently, he had been found by one of his friends on Sunday afternoon. Obviously, they knew that foul play was involved, but they had no leads as of this morning when the most recent article had been updated. They were stumped. I was relieved.

I took the laptop inside and put it in my filing cabinet. If Gayle was successful in getting Logan to take her to dinner, that would be the perfect time for me to destroy the computer. I pulled out my other laptop and took it outside with me. It was time for me to start looking for my next targets. My search would begin with finding someone to do something good for. The stories always initially upset me, but trying to figure out how to make their lives better was fun. The good stuff was also significantly more difficult to arrange than the bad stuff.

It occurred to me that I had a friend from college who still did some volunteer work at a homeless shelter. Perhaps she would know someone who would fit the profile I was looking for. I ran inside to get my phone from the bedroom. I opened up the contacts to find her name. I hadn't called her in a long time. I hoped that she hadn't changed her number.

When I opened the contact list I noticed something odd. In the first slot was an entry labeled "1A1A." I opened the entry to see a phone number with a 205 area code. My heart sank. It had to be Chris' number. He must have found this phone and entered his number. The "1A1A" was to make sure that it was first in my contact list.

I walked back through the house to the patio. I couldn't stop staring at the number. Finally, after thinking about Gayle taking her big step today, I decided to take one of my own. I hit the button to call him.

The phone rang twice before he answered. "Chris Benson."

"Hey Chris, it's me." I wanted to see if he would know my voice. I desperately wanted him to recognize me just by my voice.

The other end of the line was eerily quiet for what felt like an eternity. "Charity? Is that you? Please tell me it's you!"

"It's me, but I need to be honest with you. My name's not Charity." I stopped there. I wanted to make sure he wasn't going to hang up on me before I went any further.

He laughed. "I didn't think it was. I don't care what your name is. I'm just glad you called."

"I wasn't going to." I didn't see any reason to lie to him about it. "I'm not sure why I changed my mind. Are you busy? Have you got time to talk?"

EPILOGUE

Dear Reader,

My parents were killed by a drunk driver on their way home from their anniversary party. They had stopped on the side of the road to help another driver having car trouble. My father, mother, and the other motorist were standing between their vehicles, talking when the drunk driver hit my father's car. His car had been pushed forward and had pinned all three of them between the two vehicles. The drunk driver and my mother had been killed instantly. My father suffered severe injuries that resulted in massive internal bleeding. He died at the hospital an hour after he arrived. The driver of the vehicle that was having trouble was the only survivor. He is now paralyzed from the waist down.

The only relief I found in the entire situation was that I had told my parents that I loved them before they left the party. I found out about the accident while I was finishing up the party clean up. My father was already dead by the time I got the phone call. Gayle had been with me. Most of what happened after the call was still a blur. I didn't even try to recall those lost hours. It was still too difficult. My therapist said it wasn't healthy to block it out. He had no idea that it may be one of my healthiest coping mechanisms.

It was during the funeral services that I had decided to change my path in life. I sat and listened to stories from their friends about all of the good things that my parents had done in their lives. Charity work had been a passion of theirs. I wanted to continue that legacy. I wanted to know that what I was doing with my life would make them proud.

I thought about it for a few months before deciding exactly how I was going to live up to their expectations. I couldn't simply do superficial charity work. It was meaningless on a personal level. Very few people were drastically helped by random donations to large organizations. My parents expected more from me, and I knew it.

It was obvious simply from the name they had given me when I was born.

I am Karma. The name listed on my birth certificate is Karma Justice Sanborn. I hated my name as a child. I had been teased mercilessly for it. As an adult, I am embracing it.

Made in the USA
Middletown, DE
12 November 2018